BETWEEN HEAVEN AND EARTH

BETWEEN HEAVEN AND EARTH

Between Heaven and Earth

Conversations with American Christians

by
Helmut Thielicke

Translated and edited by
John W. Doberstein

JAMES·CLARKE & CO. LTD.
31 Queen Anne's Gate, London SW1

FOR
JULIUS H. BODENSIECK
a faithful, selfless, and unforgotten
friend of the Christians in Germany
during the hard years after 1945

Contents

vii

Translator's Note

These chapters are a small part of the fruit of Helmut Thielicke's visit to the United States in 1963, a selection from a full notebook of conversations and discussions of questions which arose both spontaneously and in response to sermons and lectures to many different kinds of audiences. The answers are not casual and unstructured, but they are also not academically framed. Though they are carefully reasoned and sometimes, it may seem to the American mind, exhaustive (since there are no simple answers to hard questions), they are warm, pastoral, existential, always concerned with the person who asks the question.

The questions are not synthetic. They present problems that trouble every thinking layman and minister and student. Pastors encounter them repeatedly in their ministry. The questions concerning the inspiration of the Bible, historical criticism, and the more recent aggravation of the problems of interpretation, detonated by Bultmann's program of demythologizing and hermeneutics, are discussed in a lucid and rewarding way, often with flashes of humor.

Helmut Thielicke has made and will continue to make a unique contribution to the American theological dialogue. His conversations with conservative evangelicals and fundamentalists are a case in point. Who else has been able to speak, and be listened to with respect and gratitude, to avant-garde scholars and to earnest fundamentalists? Is this not an ecumenical contribution, a contribution to intramural ecumenicity, so often blemished by a pride which is content to allow a wall of partition to divide us?

The chapter on racial integration is a refreshing and challenging discussion of this problem in American life from the point of view of an "outsider" who is bound by his Christian convictions and yet unwilling to judge and pontificate in a situation in which he does not have to live and share. The discussion of the Nazi regime, an illuminating and deeply moving account of life under that totalitarian tyranny, enlivened by the author's own experience as a preacher and pastor in the midst of it, constitutes in my opinion a prime document for any full-orbed understanding of that terrible phenomenon of our time.

Again the translator wishes to express his appreciation of the author's willingness to confide in him the responsibility for making editorial decisions in the preparation of this English version of his work.

JOHN W. DOBERSTEIN

A Brief Orientation for the Reader

The journey on which the following conversations took place extended across the whole of the North American continent from Los Angeles to New York, from Texas to Chicago. It took place upon invitation of numerous universities and churches. Almost every day I found myself at a lectern or in a pulpit, not infrequently several times each day. As a rule the lectures extended over several days in each city; at the University of Chicago they extended over two months. In all I was on the march for almost six months. It was my second visit to the United States; the first was in 1956.

It is impossible in brief compass to indicate even the high points of this journey. I mention only one event, because it occurred during this time: the assassination of President Kennedy. It was only a short time previously that I had delivered some lectures and enjoyed a delightful hospitality in Dallas where he died. Two days after his death I conducted a service in the chapel at Harvard University, where he and his brothers had studied and the memory of the family was especially vivid. I shall not forget the solemn dignity of that hour.

On such a journey there is naturally occasion for many discussions and conversations—at meetings of faculties, with students (with these above all; they were almost insatiable!) with whites and Negroes, with pastors and generals (I preached at a service for the military in the Pentagon), with newsmen and television personnel. There was never any lack of variety in themes and participants in the dialogue.

I was constantly accompanied by my young American secretary, Darrell Guder of Hollywood, California. He studied with us in the University of Hamburg and lived in our home for several months in preparation for the journey. It was he who helped me carry on the conversations, since my English was too weak to stand on its own feet. Thus, after having delivered a lecture or sermon in English, I was able to use my mother tongue in the discussion and express myself quite freely. We soon learned to work together so well that every little phrase and clause was swiftly translated by Darrell and the listeners were hardly conscious that the initial language was alien to them. We called it "playing ping-pong"; for as we stood before our listeners, throwing the ball to each other, their faces kept bobbing back and forth, from one to the other. It was a very amusing sight.

About the conversational situation in America: I always felt it to be an attractive and sympathetic thing that the listeners seemed to be trying to encourage one and make one feel that they were kindly disposed. One had the feeling that they were listening with a real expectation, that one would have to put one's foot in it very badly indeed to evoke a derogatory criticism. In Germany one often has the opposite impression as a speaker, namely, that one is at first received with skepticism and that a positive attitude is something that must be earned. Naturally, this too is not without its stimulation (but is perhaps more taxing!).

I enjoyed most of all the conversations with students. They are less intellectual than German students, perhaps somewhat more naïve and therefore also more "original." They come less with reflected problems acquired from reading, which are not yet rooted in their own existence, than with their personal and very genuine problems. And when it is necessary to traverse some rather complicated and theoretical terrain to get to their solution, they are quite ready to go along. It is absurd to think that they are interested only in practicalities.

I really enjoyed it when they gathered around me informally, sitting on the floor in American fashion or on the grass in the warmer fields of California and Texas. To look into these young, open, and thoughtful faces was inspiring and it drove away all feelings of fatigue.

Naturally, the conversation frequently led to some definitely and deeply insistent theological discussions, especially when they had been preceded by a corresponding lecture. In independent conversations, however, I noted, in contrast to talks with German students, how strongly these young people are concerned with questions of practical piety. Again and again questions such as these were asked: What must I do to become a Christian? How can I know that I believe? What assurances are there that I will continue to believe? How can we be sure of faith? How can we develop a regular prayer life?

About the piety of American Christians: I experienced piety as a total phenomenon here for the first time. At this point we Germans are far more critical and reserved. The attacks of dialectical theology upon subjective experience, upon all pious psychologism, are still having their effect among us, producing a kind of allergy to anything that might even remotely look like Pietism. In this respect we have probably thrown out the child with the bath and not only attacked the propensity to emotionalism but also have impugned the spiritual life itself. We have robbed it of the spontaneity of its expression; we have taken from it its naïve naturalness. On the theoretical level we are enormously concerned with the question of how Christ can be related to our existence and to everything that occupies us in this life. But we are shy of doing this in the presence of others and of allowing it to find expression, say, in common or free prayer.

Seeing these easy, natural practices among American Christians, I have come to feel that this is a lack among us. I attended hardly a single meeting where there was no prayer. Even the prior of a Catholic monastery who was welcomed as a guest in a theological colloquium was called upon, and without hesitation he obliged. One can imagine the inhibitions we would have in such a situation —to say nothing of how the prior would have squirmed!

It may be that the average American theology as it exists among the clergy and the congregations and finds expression in sermons is relatively unconcerned about the theological problems that emerge when we think through the relationship of the gospel to culture, philosophy, and society (though here the race question appears to be producing a break-through). The American Christian who prays in every life situation is nevertheless aware of this affinity of Christ to every situation of existence, probably in a much more unreflected, naïve, and less theoretical way, but therefore on a more immediate spiritual level.

At first I was somewhat disappointed that my chief work, the *Theological Ethics*,[1] was not the first to be published in the United States, but that I was rather introduced by a number of volumes of sermons and essays. I soon observed, however, that this order of things was far more helpful as far as my trip was concerned than I, in my human shortsightedness, had anticipated. These books prepared the way for a certain spiritual trust with which my hearers approached me. Moreover, they prevented my work from being given a premature theological label and pigeonholed in a particular school of thought. So people of all denominations and theological tendencies were apparently ready to listen to me. The liberals probably thought: He speaks in modern style, so he must be one of us; the Baptists said: He has written a book on Spurgeon, so he is close to us; the fundamentalists noted that my sermons were expositions of biblical texts and often included me in their ranks; and the Lutherans said: After all, he comes from Hamburg, *ergo*. . . . And so it was with the other denominations too. Again and again I had the feeling of being in a large, familiar family and of being in a higher sense "at home." It may well have been because of this constellation of circumstances that my hearers often came together, perhaps for the first time, from situations beyond the

[1] The first two volumes will be published in the spring of 1965 by Fortress Press, Philadelphia. A part of the later volumes, *The Ethics of Sex*, was published at the end of my trip to America by Harper & Row, New York.

existing barriers. I have been gratefully aware of this ecumenical outcome.

The following conversations make it apparent that I was conscious of having a special responsibility when I met with evangelicals and fundamentalists, and that I believe that one of the crucial questions that will affect the destiny of American Christianity is whether and how it comes to terms with them. I have gratefully and respectfully noted that the evangelicals and fundamentalists in this country want to preserve the substance of the Christian faith and that not infrequently they are the most dependable and self-sacrificial members of their congregations. But I have also observed with sadness how often they are criticized from the high horse of Enlightenment and then, naturally, they are unfairly dealt with.

I have given much thought to the question of how one can help the fundamentalists; for that one must help them was clear to me. They must be freed from many repressions and above all from the dichotomy of their life. But this dare not be done with a superior intellectual attitude of knowing better; for then they put up their defenses and lose the openness of trust, because they imagine the "ancient foe" is on the other side. One can talk with them only by speaking on the basis of the same faith and showing them that they are in danger of losing the very thing they want to gain.

I do not wish to anticipate here; the first dialogues will indicate how I tried to speak with them. It is a bit awkward that the very first dialogue begins rather abruptly and departs from the ordinary style of conversation. It had to be first, however, for practical reasons. The observant reader will surely discover why it was not a specifically "American" conversation, even though the interlocutor was a fundamentalist.

A comment which gave me the greatest satisfaction after one such discussion was made by a student pastor. He said, "You have freed the fettered and bound the wandering spirits." This is certainly overstated, but it rightly expresses the intention I had in mind. The same is true of another reaction expressed by one person as we were taking leave: "You have disturbed our peace and upset our doubts."

Perhaps the sealed orders I carried with me on this journey were that I should speak with the fundamentalists in this way. For perhaps only a person who comes from the outside and cannot be classified in some fixed position can count upon a certain willingness to listen to what he has to say. And so I want to say very explicitly that I found brothers in the faith in these circles.

American fundamentalists, with some exceptions, of course, are different from many German representatives of this group in that they are relaxed, altogether human, endowed with humor, and willing to listen (when they have learned to trust a person). Conversations with them were most successful after they had first listened to a sermon and had sensed that we were standing on common ground. Then they were quite willing to have theological comments made on the sermon and to consider whether *on* this common ground they need to change the direction of their march.

If American Christianity loses these people, who are often the most vital members of its body—if it should, say, drive them into sectarianism and thus allow them to die away—this could be fatal to its cause. Therefore, wherever it was possible, I tried to call attention to these questions and blow the horn as loud as I could.

Now a word with regard to the form of the dialogues. They hardly took place in the literal form in which they are printed here. They are not based on tape recordings and stenographic transcriptions, but rather on the comprehensive notes which I wrote down after each occasion. For the sake of conciseness, I have in most cases summarized a number of conversations.

I had noted down about thirty questions which cropped up again and again. Actually I had intended to deal with all of them here, since they were obviously typical and to that extent characteristic of the intellectual situation. In order not to allow this book to bulk too large, however, I have selected only a few theological and political questions. For the time being I have left out the large contingent of spiritual questions and preaching problems, though it was hard for me to do this and my notes tempted me to present these conversations too. Perhaps this may be done at a later time.

The reader will note in the various conversations that they took place on quite different levels; sometimes the interlocutors were laymen untrained in theology and sometimes they were academically trained ministers and theologians. My concern was always to allow the "contours" of my partner in the conversation to emerge as clearly as possible. My purpose was not to discuss the theological themes "as such"; I wanted rather, and was obliged, to speak in each case in a very definite direction and to particular positions.

I would think that these conversations in their present form might be useful in study and discussion groups. America is a land of discussion, and to me it would be a pleasant thought if by way of this book I might be a continuing participant in these dialogues.

BETWEEN HEAVEN AND EARTH

LIFE WITH TRANSCENDENCE

I

The Bible and God

THE QUESTION OF VERBAL INSPIRATION

QUESTION: Are there errors in the Bible?

ANSWER: You will excuse me if I seem to be somewhat floored by this question and do not answer it at once. For the fact is that I have never heard the question put in this form and am familiar with it at most in the history of theology in connection with the doctrine of verbal inspiration as it was frequently put forward in the seventeenth and eighteenth centuries. Would you be good enough to tell me a little more precisely what you mean by your question?

QUESTIONER: I believe that the Bible is God's Word. Therefore it cannot err. I had the impression that you regard some things in the Bible as being "bound to their time." Once that kind of thing begins, criticism breaks everything down. That's why I want from you a clear statement: Does the Bible contain errors or not? Please answer Yes or No!

ANSWER: Allow me first to ask you another question: Have you studied theology? This, after all, was supposed to be a meeting of ministers who have had theological training. In order to give you an answer I must know what I can assume as far as your background is concerned.

QUESTIONER: No, I have not studied theology. I am, indeed, a minister, but I attended a Bible School for a short time in England and am now delivering lectures in the United States just as you

1

are doing. But, quite frankly I do not understand the purpose of your question. I asked you to answer my question with a plain Yes or No. One certainly does not need to have studied theology to understand a Yes or a No.

ANSWER: Quite so. But the study of theology may be very useful to enable one to understand whether a question can be answered with a Yes or No at all. If you have asked me whether I am willing —to use the words of the *Heidelberg Catechism*—to confess Jesus Christ "as my only comfort in life and in death," I would have been glad to answer you in terms of simple alternatives. But you asked a *theological* question, which must be answered in a way that must make differentiations. The purpose of my question with regard to your training was to determine whether I could assume a degree of understanding of a reply that makes certain distinctions. In other words, a simple Yes or No need by no means be evidence of a simple faith (which to me is of very great importance!); it may also be so crude that it bespeaks intellectual laziness and, for my taste, may even border upon denial. A person who cultivates his simplicity in order to escape the toils and the hazards of the search for truth is not being exactly respectful to the testimonies to the truth. And the consequence may be that he may also be simply following the law of least resistance.

QUESTIONER: Yes or No, please. [Considerable murmuring among the audience.]

ANSWER: Please note very clearly that I will not allow myself to be subjected to the pressure of a false and oversimplified way of putting the question. [Restrained murmurs and nods of approval from the audience.] One of the elementary teachings of any theological education is that one must first examine the question, for the very simple reason that every question already contains within itself a meaning which prejudges the possible scope of the answer given to it. Sometimes the way in which a question is put can show that a person is looking for an answer in a direction which is completely wrong. Then the questioner must first be urged to allow himself to be put on the *right* path in asking his questions. Comparing something that is small with something very great, if you examine the pastoral dialogues of Jesus from this point of view, you will find that almost never did he give a simple answer to a question put to him, but rather replied with a counterquestion. In this way he compelled his interlocutor for one thing to change radically the *direction* in which he asked his question.

QUESTION BY ANOTHER LISTENER: I believe that for all of us it is not a pleasant thing to witness the situation into which you must now regard yourself as having been maneuvered. After all, it is exactly this relationship of question and answer, or better, question and counterquestion, in the pastoral dialogues of Jesus which has been repeatedly clarified for us in your meditations during the last few days.[1] At any rate I must confess that I really learned this and will take it away with me. Nevertheless, I would like to try and bring our discussion back to the point. If I rightly understood the Rev. Mr. X [the questioner], his question was whether the Bible and the Word of God are identical.

ANSWER: That is actually the decisive differentiation on which the answer depends, and to that I can give an answer. Naturally, we cannot here present a complete "doctrine of the Scriptures." In order to do this we would have to discuss the relation of Word and Spirit, Scripture and tradition, and church and canon. When we proceed to select a few partial questions out of this whole complex—and certainly I cannot do more than that here—we must necessarily speak in terms that may not always be guarded. Allow me to state only two points with regard to this question of how the Bible and the Word of God relate to each other.

First: In Holy Scriptures the great acts and messages of God are proclaimed to us. They tell us that we come from him, with all that we are and have; but that we have become unfaithful to our origin and the purpose for which we were created and have

---

[1] The author had been giving a series of interpretations of New Testament passages on these conversations of Jesus with inquirers.

gone off into a far country. They also tell us that God wants to bring us back home, to our salvation, and they tell us what he has expended and sacrificed in order to bring us to this his goal. This, as we have said before, is the *theme* of the Holy Scriptures. And we live by allowing the Scriptures to say this to us. For it is they alone that "bear witness" to this.[2]

Second: God communicates this to us by calling men into his service, by attesting himself to them, and by dealing with them. He makes them his peculiar instruments. This peculiar and special way in which he deals with those whom he has appointed to be bearers of his revelation is nowhere more beautifully expressed than in the account which says that the Lord used to speak to Moses "as a man speaks to his friend."[3]

Thus the Bible gives us an account of a living history, a living encounter of living men with the living God. These men are constantly failing and falling down in this history; they misunderstand God, they are unfaithful to him, they go off on many wrong paths, and in exactly this way they have ever new experiences of the faithfulness of God, who holds fast to them despite everything. It is not only the believing *man* who says to God, "Nevertheless I am continually with thee," when God's way seems to lead into darkness and his footprints disappear in the waters; *God* also speaks to man and says, "Nevertheless—even though you are what you are—I am continually with thee."[4] One might even say that God also says to Jacob, "I will not let you go until I have blessed you."[5]

Here this faithfulness of God is by no means an anthropomorphic expression for an indifferent metaphysical principle that stands unmoved above the antitheses of faith and unbelief, good and evil, embracing them all beyond all polarity. On the contrary, this is an exceedingly dynamic faithfulness: here we are dealing with the history of a living heart. One has only to consult

[2] John 5:39. Cf. 5:37 and 8:18.
[3] Exod. 33:11.
[4] Ps. 73:23 ff.; 77:19.
[5] Gen. 32:26 ff.

a concordance of the Bible to see all the examples of how God can "repent" his ever having had anything to do with man with all his instability and egotistical cupidity, and then how he himself is sorry for this angry regret.

So here we are dealing not with the timeless principle of pure immutability, but rather with the affirmation that God bows down to enter into a *history* with us, that he is altogether "personal," and that in goodness and severity he participates in all the ups and downs of our life story.

In the form in which the Bible speaks of God's emotions, this may in fact often sound anthropomorphic. But the thing itself, the movement of God's heart, the "history in God," is by no means anthropomorphic. Anybody who nevertheless insists that it is anthropomorphic is simply missing the point of what happens to us in Jesus Christ. For it becomes completely clear, or better, here it actually happens, here it becomes an "event," that God enters into our history, that he gives himself up to the temptation and the suffering of human existence and takes his stand at our side in full solidarity when he subjects himself *with us* to his judgment and descends into every depth into which we are dragged. How else can one understand the Cross of Calvary except that here God's holiness is in conflict with his grace: he does not simply pass over man's sin lightly, but rather throws himself into it, casts himself into the balance, by "giving his only begotten Son." Golgotha is a pain in God's heart. And even at the risk of its again sounding anthropological (or mythological!) I would say that this is a God overcoming himself, this is a struggle of God with himself. So emphatically is this the story of a living heart.

The slightest deviation from this thesis leads immediately to the idea of a "divine principle," and thus into a wilderness where living faith can no longer grow. Here we must be in dead earnest about the mighty acts of God. It is not merely a matter of the "divine law" of an event; rather God *does* something. He speaks, and it comes to be. And in that he speaks and acts, he determines and decides. Therefore his action never lies on the level of our postulates; he acts upon us in the name of his freedom. Therefore we are confronted with his sovereign will.

Because he thus enters into a history with us, he moves the hearts of his servants and is not content merely to guide their pen or goose quill for them. This is actually the way in which the advocates of the doctrine of verbal inspiration conceived it to have happened. What this was, expressed in modern terms, was a fantastic idea of a heavenly cybernetics in which God was the guide of a process of automatic writing.

But it is not the fantastic side of this conception that bothers me here. There is a sense in which we cannot get along without the category of the fantastic in matters of faith, at least when we mean by it the fact that God's speech and action, his working as the Lord of history and our own life history, lie beyond all that we can think or imagine. The Christian is and always will be an adventurer, who can never make long-range plans, but rather waits for God's decisions. He therefore expects that his own projects may be sovereignly thwarted and is content with the "lamp for our feet,"[6] which illumines only the next step and allows him to walk like a child in the darkness.

The fantastic as such therefore need not necessarily frighten us off when we consider the idea that God guided the quills of the biblical writers and caused them to set down not only the Hebrew consonants but also—as was likewise affirmed—the subscribed vowels. (In a way this postulate concerning the consonants and vowels is even rather impressive, since it shows that these people of the older Orthodoxy at least had the courage to think an idea through to the end and be consistent.)

There is something else about this notion, however, which is far more alarming, and that is that it leads to a *legalistic* attitude toward the Holy Scriptures. How could I go on hearing in, and accepting from, a Scripture which came into being in this way the message of God's free grace, the message that I am his free child,

[6] Ps. 119:105.

when at every step I am forced to "repress" something, forced to interpret and allegorize a meaning into the obscure passage, because, after all, it is *God* who has written this? How could I go on feeling that I have been called into God's saving history, how could I go on thinking of myself as a spiritual son of the "fathers in the faith," as a fellow citizen with all the saints, if the messages on the basis of which I am to do this are themselves not a part of this "history," if it is no longer a matter of living testimony through living witnesses at all, but only of a book that has fallen from heaven? How then could there be any possibility of faith as trust? How could one avoid falling into a very slavish obedience, an obedience which would be just as mechanical as the way in which this Book is said to have come into being, an obedience which would be totally mechanical and indiscriminate, which would simply say yea and amen to everything without ever entering into a living dialogue with God in which decisions are made? Does God take any pleasure in this kind of slavish obedience (and all the repression and compulsion that goes with it)? Is this really doing justice to what he has done precisely in order to call us *away* from all servitudes and make us free children who learn to say "Abba, Father" with the spontaneity of a child? Where have we gotten to with all this?

Then there is something else connected with living faith which becomes impossible when we cling to this mechanical theory and that is that we can no longer distinguish within the Bible between that which it proclaims to us for our salvation *and* the contemporary means of expression which it uses to do this. For, naturally, these means of expression are conditioned by the time in which they were uttered. The scholar has little difficulty in seeing that the biblical account of creation, with all its differences from the mythical cosmogonies, employs some of the conceptual elements of these myths—such as those of Babylonian and Assyrian origin. It makes use, so to speak, of the pictorial material that exists in these human conceptions. But it takes the mosaic stones of these pictorial elements and constructs a completely *new* picture. It forces the pictorial language of myth into its service (just as it does with the vocabulary of ancient philosophy, for example, in the case of the term Logos). And in doing so it renders powerless the *message* of those myths from which it takes these images. The Bible uses the myths and at the same time demythologizes them. So it also uses the cosmological concepts of its time. It would certainly be frightfully foolish to demand of the Bible a post-Copernican cosmology just so that it would prove itself to be the infallible Word of God! Naturally for the author of the first two chapters of the Bible the earth is a flat disk arched over by the glassy globe of the firmament.

Is not all of this the very sign of the miracle of the "humanity" of God—the sign that he makes his Word become flesh and that he comes into our history? This surely means that he wants to come and meet us where we are, just as the servants of the king in the parable went out into the market place, the highways, and the hedges in order to fetch the guests for the royal wedding.[7] And the fact that he wants to find us, that he follows us into the far country, surely means that he wants to be right where we are, that he addresses us in our own language and "accommodates" himself to us. We can pray to him in our own language—no matter whether it be English, German, or Hottentot—and we can also hear his Word in our language.

Thus every generation brings out particular emphases of the message, because every generation is sought out and met by God at different points, in different ways of putting the question, and in different needs. This is also the reason why we cannot simply recite the famous old sermons in our pulpits, even though we know that Augustine or Luther or Wesley were far better preachers than we are. No, God wants to meet us on *our* streets and *our* lanes. In the atomic age we have to say these things in a different way from the way they had to be said in the sixteenth century. We have to say them differently simply because in our day too

[7] Matt. 22:1-14. Cf. *The Waiting Father* (New York: Harper & Row, 1959), pp. 182-192.

God wants to stand beside us and speak to us in our language. Is it not therefore a wonderfully comforting thing to realize that this is what God has always done and that he uses the images and the ideas which have existed in the minds and the imaginations of men?

We certainly would deprive this message of its most decisive element if we were to ignore this gracious accommodation on the part of God, that is, if we were to put the *means* of expression God uses on the same level as that which he wishes to say with the help of these means. For then, in theological language, we would be guilty of the heresy of Docetism, we would be robbing the Word of God of its fleshliness, its entry into history, and making of it a superearthly, timeless, and pseudocorporeal phantom.

Perhaps you have noted that in this polemic against the doctrine of verbal inspiration I have not used a single rationalistic argument. I have not said, for example, that this doctrine is so contradictory to the way we would rationally conceive of a written document coming into being that it constitutes too great a demand upon our reason. I would consciously dismiss such arguments myself, because reason can neither provide a basis for our faith nor take it away from it. I have also refrained from operating with the argument that our knowledge of how the biblical texts actually came into being makes it impossible for us to accept the idea of such an unhistorical dictating mechanism. This does not mean that I would simply brush aside this latter argument as irrelevant and immaterial. On the contrary, there are two reasons why I consider it to be altogether relevant and not something that one can snobbishly and pharisaically dismiss as rationalistic.

The *first* reason is that God, who has himself entered into the history of man, has by that token also sanctioned our historical concern with that history. Certainly it is impossible to say, "The Word became flesh" and "The Lord took on the form of a servant and entered into our history," and then immediately add, "But do not look at me too closely! Do not examine the 'flesh' and investigate the history! You must either accept the whole historical package unopened, accept the whole of it in faith just as it is handed out to you in this Book, or you have disowned me in unbelief." I repeat: God, who wants to meet us in history—not in history in general, but in *his* history—has thereby sanctioned the historical study of that history.

This statement is not at all contradictory to the fact that man is capable of pursuing this historical work on the history in a very godless and disobedient way, that he may, for example, seek in that history the confirmation of his own preconceived ideas (Hegel and Marx are only two of numberless examples), or that he may turn the condescension of God into a derogation of God by saying that this was not a case of the Logos having become flesh, but rather of the flesh having invented a Logos for itself. It would be a remarkable thing if man's sinfulness and self-sufficiency had seeped into all the works of man, but not into his *historical* work! Just as there is such a thing as a receptive and reflective reason (and not merely a rationalism that has run wild), so there is a kind of historical study based upon faith which explores the servant form of the Word of God and gratefully notes its accommodation (and which is therefore not a historicism that relativizes everything).

The *second* reason why I consider the reference to the historical origin of the biblical texts as theologically essential is that the regard for truth dare never become greater outside the church than it is in the church. What do we mean by that?

When I cling to the mechanistic doctrine of verbal inspiration I push the historical question out of the realm of faith and thus leave it to unbelief. And anybody who has even a little knowledge of the history of ideas knows what unbelief proceeds to do with this question and what happens to it "outside the gate."[8] But we who think we are in the sanctuary and that we are serving God by refusing to have anything to do with the historical question are dishonoring the truth in an even more brutal way; we are

[8] Heb. 13:12.

actually suppressing the truth. We are afraid that the historical truth which we may possibly discover will compromise our faith and thus become a danger to it.

Thus the very thing which at first may look like an act of faith, a sacrifice of the intellect, turns out to be nothing more than lack of faith. It would be pure fear, the foolish policy of sticking one's head in the sand, a betrayal of him who is the King of truth. How can anybody who is on the outside believe at all, if we proclaim the King of truth and at the same time are afraid that the first good historical discovery will expose him as a false king, an ordinary man dressed up like a king, or a projection of human fantasy?

But this would only be one side of our attempted assassination of the truth. The other would be that we would be denying an elementary effect of the truth of God, namely, that it makes us "free,"[9] delivers us from all fear,[10] and gives us the freedom of a child to move about in the Father's house. A person who has to repress things is really afraid and is by no means free. He is stuffed with complexes. In normal life he may be wide wake and critical, regarded as a sober businessman, a coolly objective engineer, a realistic newspaper reporter (who cannot be hoodwinked), but in the "religious sector" of his life he audibly shifts into another gear. Here he closes his eyes, and in this way he proceeds to "believe blindly." Here he looks away from things instead of at them. Here he faces taboos, and instead of being one who has been liberated by the Word, he becomes an idolater of the Word-fetish.

The result is a kind of spiritual schizophrenia, a split personality, which compels him to live in two strictly separated realms. Do you think that God takes any pleasure in this spiritual illness of his children, these cramping complexes, when, after all, his will is to make them free? Do you think that God enjoys having to look at the way we are willing to surrender only one side, the "pious" side, of our lives to him (but at what a price and in what form!), while we think we can go on all the more undisturbed

---

[9] John 8:32.
[10] Luke 1:74.

being objective and this-worldly in the other area, the "secular" realm? Certainly this not only perverts the "religious sector" but also makes the "secular realm" godless by the attempt to keep it out of the realm of God's sovereignty.

We see, then, that the rational and historical arguments which can be directed against the doctrine of verbal inspiration are by no means merely rationalistic in character. They are by no means merely arguments with which a person tries to prove his own intellectual skill and thus seeks to evade the claim of the eternal Word. In any case, we must not allow ourselves to be frightened by the observation that it is possible to polemicize against theological positions even in this *questionable* way and then conclude that whenever anyone raises the question of truth at all (and then quite naturally must speak of the responsibility of reason), whenever anyone even brings up the historical problem, he has already deserted the cause and no longer stands within the obedience of faith. I would think that we have now seen how faith and reason interrelate with each other here and therefore how sadly we deny our faith if at *any* point we evade or prejudice the truth.[11]

I have therefore tried at every point in my answer not to be "rationalistic" in the cheap sense, saying to the questioner: My dear friend, you will need only a modicum of historical and philosophical education to make you feel that the doctrine of verbal inspiration is an intellectual monstrosity and cause you to abandon it with horror. I believe that I (or better, an expert biblical scholar) could have enormously embarrassed my esteemed interlocutor by enumerating some very simple historical facts. I have not, however, made the slightest attempt to do this, not at all because my good manners forbid it, but above all because it would have led us away from our real theme. I wanted rather to lead to the theme and to show quite simply that verbal inspiration is not primarily in conflict with "reason" and "history" but with faith

[11] On the relation of reason and faith compare the chapter on "the freedom of reason over against the world (a theological 'critique of reason')" in *Theologische Ethik*, II, 1, §1321 ff.

itself, namely, that it denies the gracious condescension of God into our history, that it denies his accommodation to us, the incarnation of the Word, and besides that it must necessarily, because of its little faith, repress the question of truth and defame the work of the historical scholar as being antigod. Thus this doctrine actually allows the concern for truth to be greater *outside* the church than *in* the church. And besides, it intensifies the untruth "outside the gate."

I have therefore warned the advocates of verbal inspiration, not against having too much faith (this would be another question), but rather against having too little faith. I have therefore *consciously* refrained from putting myself on any other level than that on which the adherents of this doctrine wish to stand. I have not posed as one who is supposedly more enlightened theologically and historically and railed at a naïve faith. Rather, as one who wants to believe *along with* his interlocutor, I have wished to warn against piously disguised unbelief and to appeal for a deepening of faith. I would put to my interlocutor, who obviously presented his question whether the Bible contains any errors from the point of view of verbal inspiration, this counterquestion, whether he can really serve the faith, which he wants to serve, by means of this theory and whether this does not involve him in a profound self-contradiction.

Therefore my answer was intended, not to be polemical, but rather the word of a brother, though he really did not treat me very kindly. I wanted to oppose in the name and on the basis of faith the legalism, which comes in by the back door, disguised in a pious mask and posing as an "angel of light," and threatens to break down everything that is precious to us in the gospel. I hope that my fundamentalist brethren (for they certainly are my brethren) have noted that in everything I have said I have wished to be an advocate of the Holy Scriptures.

II

Historical Criticism of the Bible

THE HISTORICAL-CRITICAL STUDY OF THE SCRIPTURES.
A CONVERSATION WITH FUNDAMENTALISM

QUESTION: I belong, with not a few others who are here this after-
noon, to those who come from a fundamentalist background.
Therefore what you said yesterday with regard to the doctrine of
verbal inspiration was rather disturbing for me. Naturally, I shall
have to give it some further thought. One cannot deal with it all
at once. But I believe that already I can see that something liberating has come out of your presentations. I do not know for sure
whether this will be the case with me, but what makes me feel
free to think about what you have said is the feeling that you are
not interested in freeing us to be uncommitted but rather that you
want to call us to a deeper commitment of faith. You want to
release us, as it were, from a wrong kind of bondage. Hitherto I
have heard only "liberal" attacks upon my fundamentalism. That
is to say, these attacks came from people who were also cutting
away at all the other tenets of our doctrine and to whom the
advances of science and general knowledge seemed to be more
important than humbly holding fast to the spiritual heritage be-
queathed to us by our fathers. Perhaps the rest of your listeners
have had the same experience, but at any rate I must confess that
this is the first time I ever heard anyone dispute the central doctrine of fundamentalism, that is, the doctrine of verbal inspiration,
not in the name of unbelief, but rather of faith, and at the same
time say that in doing this his purpose was to uphold the Holy
Scriptures as the sole source of revelation. This goes to the heart,
this a man can listen to without immediately having to feel that

he is denying his faith even by listening to it. Therefore what you have said has been a liberation for me. Sometimes I even had the feeling that you knew me, though this is quite impossible. I felt, for example, that you were talking about my own spiritual conflicts when you said that as long as one believes in the doctrine of verbal inspiration all kinds of things have to be repressed and one dare not let the question of truth get too close to you. I deeply love the Bible and I study it constantly. I would also like to read commentaries. But I am always afraid that they will get me mixed up and take my faith away from me. Otherwise I am a young man who is close to life, and I have kept very careful tabs on the contractor who built our church ["Good for you!"—exclamation from the audience, folowed by laughter indicating approval], but in this matter I am very timid. Many times I have exactly the same feeling which you described, of living in two different compartments. And this never seemed to me to be quite honest. I merely wanted to say this to you, that you might see that your words have fallen on receptive soil. But you certainly will also understand that one cannot immediately rush over to your position with flying colors, but must first digest it. Yet I have the feeling that something has been set in motion, that a certain tension has been relaxed, and that I no longer have to hold on to something by main force, but rather can examine the question calmly. [Again expressions of approval from the audience.]

So, even though I need time to work this through, I would like to ask you something. For now we've got you here and we never know when an angel will come again to these parts to trouble the waters of the pool of Bethesda.

For the reasons stated I have not yet read Bultmann. But I have heard some horrible things about him—for example, that he regards the Gospels as nothing more than legends and myths and that he does not believe in the resurrection. And he is a historical-critical student of the Bible. You said that we do honor to the Holy Scriptures when we also take into acount its historical background, that only in this way do we respect the servant form of the Scriptures and God's gracious entrance into our history.

Theoretically, I would agree with this. But when it comes to actual practice, the picture is quite different. Then we see people like Bultmann whose work is only destructive. I know a young minister who lost his faith through reading his books and is now looking for another job. So I ask myself whether God really is in favor of the historical-critical study of the Bible. But then where are we going to draw the line between keeping our eyes open to the humanity of God and the historical transmission of his revelations on the one hand and destructive criticism on the other?

ANSWER: Thank you for your frank statement, and above all for the fact that you have caught what I have been trying to do, namely, that what I am interested in is respect for the Word of God and not its depreciation or relativization.

The depth and honesty of your reaction has again shown me how much of the best, but frozen, spiritual capital of the church is to be found in its fundamentalist members. Everywhere I see they belong to the faithful and steady part of the congregations and that one can depend upon them. And I am not overlooking the fact that they want to pass on the riches of faith unchanged from generation to generation and therefore do not want to expose them to the winds of every spirit of the times. They really possess a great spiritual capital. The fact that it appears indeed to be "frozen" (I hope you will not take this amiss) is certainly in many cases not to be attributed to the fact that people have been *consciously* "of little faith" and have decided upon reflection to "repress" certain things. If anything like this is the case, it certainly is more unconscious than conscious.

There are surely historical reasons why such a thing is possible. America did not pass through an age of theological "Enlightenment" in the sense that we did in the eighteenth century. It did not have a Lessing—to name only the most respected representa-

---

[1] Cf. the author's book, *Offenbarung, Vernunft und Geschichte. Studien zur Religionsphilosophie Lessings*, 4 Aufl., 1961.

tive of the German Enlightenment[1]—who so relentlessly and systematically posed the question of how one can accept faith in the absolute in the midst of the relativity of the historical and how the truth of reason and the truth of history are related to each other. This kind of searching cross-examination put so many difficulties in the way of all naïve and self-confident orthodoxy that it simply could not go on pursuing the even tenor of its way but had to come to grips with its assailants.

Thus all these problems were brought home to people in a wholly different way. It was simply impossible to go on being as naïve as it may sometimes appear to be possible in this country. (I admit again that this is humanly very attractive.) Even the Bible-believing Christians had at least to go through this barrage and could not avoid it by any kind of maneuver. Nor could they simply close their ears to these critical questions.

But in the long run *nobody* can maintain this kind of naïveté, not even American Christians. They, of all people, cannot do it because Americans, despite their idealism, are by no means mere dreamers out of touch with reality. And just because Americans are what they are, an artificially preserved life in two compartments will always lead to greater tensions and even complexes. Then Christians become obliged, at least in the "religious sphere," to shut themselves off more and more from the outside world. I am really fearful that a fundamentalism which does not keep its great spiritual capital fluid, instead of merely guarding it in the dark, will in time inevitably produce sectarian tendencies and drive the non-Christian world ever more radically into its worldliness. The hedge that separates that kind of church from the world grows higher and higher and the faith that is lived inside of it can become increasingly incredible and unacceptable to the outsider. And then what things will look like *inside* the hedge—well, I cannot talk about that now.

Because the American churches have so many fundamentalists and because these hold in their hands an essential portion of their spiritual substance, I regard the question of how American Christianity deals with the problem of fundamentalism as nothing short of fateful for its destiny. Whether it will solve this problem and thus whether it can prevent the spread of sectarian tendencies, precisely within the circles which are most conservative, the most intent upon conserving and preserving the heritage, whether it can keep the pool of Bethesda from becoming a stagnant pond which no angel ever troubles—this depends upon *how* the conversation with the fundamentalists is carried on in the American churches.

If the fundamentalists feel that they are merely looked down upon as backward and behind the times and they are facing only the superior arrogance of rationalistic "know-it-alls," then they certainly will *not* be willing to talk with others. Then they will only be driven into obduracy. For the fact is that they are not naïve because they are "by nature" naïve and thus that they are constitutionally at odds with their contemporaries. They are naïve because they *want* to be naïve. (It is therefore an assumed naïveté.) And they want to be naïve because they believe that otherwise they will lose their faith.

This is, after all, a very honorable motive, however mistaken it may be. They are willing, as it were, to sell all they have—even a mind that is open to historical facts, even the unreserved search for the truth—in order to gain the one thing needful. How could we, how could we dare to despise this!

But, unfortunately, this is often done. Even great theologians whom I highly esteem are capable of doing this on occasion. One ought rather to see a great faithfulness at work here, which has only hardened into the holding of positions which cannot be held in this way and also should not be held at all. One can only pray to God that we may succeed in making one thing clear to the fundamentalists, namely, that we want to live together with them by those mighty acts of God, which they are trying to surround with the wrong kind of hedges. We look to the same Father's house that they do. Like them, we know that He is waiting for us there and we know *why* this is so. We would wish, however, that we might go there on the same road—which again has been prepared for us—and that we may walk in this house not as slaves going to their labor but as children to their Father.

But one can speak to fundamentalists *only* in such a way that they will know that we love them, that we do not want to lord it over their faith but rather work with them for their joy, and that we honor what they are loyally trying to preserve. But along with this love, everybody who looks at the spiritual and theological development in America with open eyes will also be motivated by a sense of responsibility for our whole generation of Christians. I repeat: judging from a human point of view, the question of how the question of fundamentalism is solved will determine the fate of American Christianity. This conclusion will not be one that contains an all too worldly philosophy of history if we realize that this is a question which is being put to us by God and no one else.

Now with regard to the question which has been directed to me, I must first say something in vindication of Ruldolf Bultmann. Allow me to state here as clearly as possible, as I have in not a few other places in this country, that many people here have a conception of him which is a complete caricature. I can say this the more impartially in that I am really anything but a "Bultmannian," in that I regard his theological approach as being extremely dubious at certain decisive points and have repeatedly stated this in a number of articles.[2] Just for this reason, however, fairness demands that I state very clearly what follows.

The very deep doctrinal differences that separate me from Bultmann dare not be a reason for me to regard him as a heretic, that is, a thinker "outside of the church." Since most of you have only heard something about him but have not read his writings, it is difficult for me to illustrate this by what he has written. [*Note*

---

[2] Cf., for example, "The Restatement of New Testament Mythology" in *Kerygma and Myth*, ed. by Hans Werner Bartsch (New York: Harper Torchbook edition, 1961), pp. 138-178.

from a later discussion. In a more extensive two-part lecture on the resurrection kerygma, which I delivered at several universities, I was able to assume a different background of understanding and thus could enter more fully into the controversy with Bultmann. In this particular discussion we were dealing with the typical situation in a gathering of American ministers. They by no means showed only a purely "practical" interest, as many European theologians believe they do, but were always thoroughly receptive to basic thinking in the area of principles. On the other hand, they were, apart from exceptions, quite understandably less familiar with the present state of discussion in German theology. In seminaries and universities the situation was often otherwise. There is, in my opinion, no recondite reason for this time lag in the discussion in this country and abroad; it would seem to me to be connected in a very simple way with the delay in translation. If it is true that it often takes two decades before the important books from my country are translated, it is only natural that the corresponding questions should gain momentum in America much later. The arrogant feeling that we are "further" along is in itself highly questionable. For as a rule these questions have not really been settled and solved so that we could go on "further." I may perhaps allow myself to say something quite heretical: In the history of theology certain problems are for the most part not settled because the problems have been solved, but rather are so thoroughly talked to death that we can no longer listen to them. We get "fed up" with them. Then we turn to other things which are likewise important, which we have forgotten in our mania for problems. (Theologians too can be terrible monomaniacs in their fixation upon certain problems!) Then after twenty years along comes another scholar who says: These problems have been lying here unsettled for decades, we must now repair the unfinished tasks of our past. Naturally, I have intentionally exaggerated this little caricature of the history of theology, but this somewhat caricatured distortion of the proportions of things expresses something which is not altogether false.]

But since Americans are not averse to statements which have a personal tone, I may perhaps try, if not to substantiate, then at least to make my position clear from this point of view. During the Third Reich Bultmann belonged to the Confessing Church. Here, where it was really hard to take a stand, he stood in the ranks of those who confessed the faith in the face of great trial. This cannot be said of many orthodoxists and pietists who today turn up their noses at him (though I am far from pronouncing any kind of general condemnation). This naturally says nothing about whether one can agree with his theology; but perhaps it may serve as a word of caution to those who are so quick to hand out charges of heresy.

Furthermore, there is only one situation in which I would really be clearly obliged to conclude that a person had separated himself from the Church of Jesus Christ and that would be if he had closed the Bible or had destroyed it by "criticism" that there was nothing left to close. This situation can occur if a person dissociates himself from the Bible on principle, or also if he has distilled from it certain ideas—say, of a moralistic kind—which then take on a "secular" or "Christian" life of their own, no longer requiring any connection with their source, or if the biblical stories are reduced, as they were by Reimarus, to a collection of crime stories and romantic tales. But a person who keeps the Bible open and reflects upon it, always remaining a listener, will always be a member of the body of Christ in one form or another.

I would say that this conclusion is not based upon a diagnosis of a particular person's faith. Who could think he was capable of making such a diagnosis, who would even undertake such a thing and thus encroach upon the prerogative of the eternal Judge! I should rather think that this judgment as to whether a person is a member of the body of Christ is in the strictest sense *itself* an article of faith. For it is sustained and upheld by our faith that the

Holy Scriptures enter into a *history* with him who has opened them and that they do not cease to carry on this history, that they do not cease verifying the affirmation that the Word of God shall no return unto him void.[3]

Bultmann and his disciples place themselves in this history. And the fact is that this history has moved *further*; never for a moment does it remain in the same place like a finished picture. On this point it is very illuminating to note that among the disciples of Bultmann, the second generation of this school, the Bible has already entered into a further stage of that history. They are now re-examining their positions in the light of the biblical message. They are finding a new way to approach the question of the historical Jesus, to the futurity of the eschaton, to history as a whole. I am not concerned at the moment to make a judgment whether this is an advance, whether this re-examination will lead to a greater closeness to the Bible. I am now merely pointing out the fact that here reflection is going on over the open Bible and that the Bible is having its history with those who thus listen to it.

Since the question addressed to me with regard to Bultmann was not so much concerned with problems of the theological discussion (for this one would have to have read what he has written) as with a spiritual concern and a spiritual distrust, it may be sufficient if at this time (as I did in many other places where the situation was exactly the same) I approach him in *this* way and attempt to dispel a number of prejudices which threaten to block an impartial hearing of the real seriousness of this theology. And having made that statement, I can also say this: I would be very unhappy and would deem it a great disaster if Bultmann's theology were to establish itself in the church. It seems to me that it leads to an existentialistic bottleneck and a resorption of theology by anthropology which gravely diminishes the riches of the message. But this opinion must never lead to the conclusion that here we are dealing with the devil, that we must burrow ourselves in as Christians, keep our fingers off it, and that the most important thing for us to do is to preserve

[3] Isa. 55:11.

the younger generation of ministers and theologians from such infections.

The exact opposite conclusion is the right one. We cannot preserve an artificial naïveté in the face of Bultmann's sharp and critical question; we cannot "play dead." This would be simply dishonest and our preaching would be robbed of its authority if we acted "as if nothing had happened" and turned back to the Reformation tradition of exegesis and preaching because it still seems to be sound and unbroken. This good Christian bread would then grow moldy in our hands and we would not be faithful and steadfast but just "reactionary." Thus when I steer toward the goal of this Reformation preaching (which as far as my personal conviction is concerned is actually what I want to do), I can do so only by facing and dealing with these problems and I find my way through to Reformation theology by overcoming this other theology.

For in this theology of Bultmann all the difficulties which the so-called "modern man" has in accepting a message which, after all, is thousands of years old, are stated and thought through. They have been weighed and thought through not because these scholars are infatuated with modern man but simply because they, like us, *belong* to this type of man and therefore have to come to terms with *themselves* because they want to find their way to saying an *honest* Yes.

Therefore one must not repress these difficulties, but rather—as in psychoanalysis, if you please—objectify them, bring them into the conscious mind, clear them up and in *this* way overcome them. But then, logically, one must also become acquainted with theology in which all this happens or at any rate should happen. Then one must not be afraid that one's faith will be endangered. Failing this, one becomes not only dishonest but one also is acting in the name of "little faith."

This is also the reason why I myself am somewhat hesitant about formulating theological antitheses to Bultmann here. For if I do this before you had read him and faced him yourself, I shall be perpetrating something in the nature of an illegitimate inoculation. I shall be helping to immunize you against something which we must allow to break out and face by ourselves.

QUESTION: Could you not say something about the general problem of historical criticism of the Bible along with the specific question concerning Bultmann?

ANSWER: Gladly—but then I would want to proceed on the same principle as we have with Bultmann. That is to say, I would prefer not to deal so much with the actual problems, but rather keep in mind my *fundamentalist* interlocutors and discuss that which in their opinion must prevent them from entering into these subjects at all.

Here we must say first of all that there may be two completely heterogeneous motives at work behind the endeavors of historical-critical study of the Bible.

The *first* motive may consist in the desire to destroy prejudices and declare war on all dogmatism. It is easy to understand that this motive gained ground especially in the period of rationalism. For that was the time when reason awakened in its normative self-consciousness, reflected upon its autonomy, and, so, to speak, caused this rational being, man, to become allergic to everything that made any claim upon him from outside himself. Because man regarded himself to be the center of vision in the whole perspective of this world, he reacted with extreme sensitiveness to everything that claimed to come from beyond this horizon and to be "supernatural." Thus there developed the passion to use reason to show that what was supposed to be supernatural was actually quite natural and to expose those who related such "irrational" or "suprarational" miracles either as superstitiously stupid or as cunning deceivers. Only in extreme cases, however, did this go so far as it did—for example, in Reimarus' passion for "debunking" which we have already mentioned.

Deeper thinkers, like Lessing, made their attack at another point. They raised the question of how the dubious trustworthiness of historical accounts (and *which* historical accounts!) could ever be adequate to supersede the far more certain truths of reason and provide a basis for the meaning and purpose of human life. Then this conviction that the truths of reason cannot be surpassed did not by any means lead (as in the case of Reimarus) simply to dismissing the truths of history as fraud, but rather to an effort to examine them for their rational content and to discover the eternal truth in its temporal garb. This is what Lessing did in his *Education of the Human Race*. But even when there was no desire simply to break the connection with historical revelation but rather to regain it by a roundabout way, the presupposition was nevertheless that everything in it that can really claim validity is only a religious and often a very mythological paraphrase of what man, the rational being, is capable of producing by himself in the way of knowledge of truth. In this way reason was elevated to the position of being the criterion of everything that claims to be the truth. And the faith of man in himself and his normative consciousness of truth took precedence as a conditioning factor over everything else that he might feel impelled to believe or think.

Under these conditions those who did not possess any special or very deep-seated tie to the Christian tradition (as Lessing, for example, did) would naturally be exposed to the temptation to break down the claims of revelation, miracle accounts, and alleged manifestations of God (often with considerable cynicism!) and to delight in the freedom which newly awakened reason had finally opened up or which they proceeded to seize upon with wide-eyed wonder. In this case men "use" the historical-critical study of the Bible for a very definite purpose—namely, in order to confirm their own intellectual presuppositions. They demolish the structure of dogma which is founded upon "historical truths" with the crowbar of historical criticism—for the greater glory of an autonomous truth of reason, which will then hold the field by itself.

It is very curious that the Christian church always remembers the "first impression" it receives of a new discovery or scientific movement. And often this first impression lives on in the church like a youthful traumatic experience. Thus the church had its first encounters with the historical-critical study of the Bible in the form of the reason-conscious rationalist. And it has not forgotten that some of these people were very callous and disrespectful and believed precious little. It then tends involuntarily to cherish a similar suspicion of the later and present-day scholars engaged in the scientific study of the Bible.

The same situation obtained with regard to the biologists who advocated the theory of descent. Among them too were a number of prominent men who set forth that doctrine with the malicious assertion that this proved that the biblical story of creation was a ridiculous fairy tale. And was it not the same with the discovery of the social question? It first appeared on the scene in a large way with the label of dialectical materialism and was raised by that atheistic bugaboo of the bourgeoisie, Karl Marx.

The same old thing happened again and again: the church of Christ suffered a shock in these first confrontations which made it largely incapable of standing up to a new problem and facing it calmly and objectively. When the same questions crop up later or elsewhere in a completely different form, its pulse goes up exactly as it did "in the month of May," it sees red or—to change the color scheme—it thinks it is again seeing the Black Man. In exactly the same way the specters of the past haunt its imagination when it hears the phrase "historical-critical study of the Bible." Here psychotherapy or pastoral care is often more needed than serious argumentation—or at any rate would have to precede it.

All this may explain why it is that many devout and honest Christian people have overlooked the fact that historical-critical Scripture research can be pursued with an entirely different motive from that of a possibly destructive Rationalism, namely, the desire to "understand" and to "appropriate" the message. This is the second motive of which I would like to speak.

Theologians of this kind are struck with a certain horror when they see people naïvely reading the Bible on the basis of their own presuppositions, completely failing to note that they are arbitrarily reading their own presuppositions into the text and thus merely turning it into an allegorical paraphrase of propositions which they already possessed. Thus it has been thought, for example, that one could read an entire Catholic, Lutheran, or Reformed orthodoxy out of the Bible. One can imagine to what extent one would have to use, not a rationalistic, but rather a "pious," traditionalistic crowbar in order to tear down what is actually there and reconstruct it according to one's own thought patterns. The dangerous thing about this is that people do not see that it is a reconstruction, as they do in the case of the "wicked freethinkers." For, after all, they undertake these manipulations with a subjectively honest respect for the Word of God and therefore allow its façades to stand: indeed, in a rather dubious way they put it under the protection of "the commission for the preservation of historical monuments."

In the face of this kind of "pious" mishandling of the Scriptures the motive of truth can drive one to investigate with all the available means of research the question: what did this biblical writer, what did Isaiah, for example, really want to say? In order to determine this one must explore the historical situation in which he spoke and one must also know the situation against which he was speaking. One must be familiar with the literary genre which he employed and the sources which he used, and also ascertain any possible reactors who had a part in producing the text as we have it today. And there are many other routines which are demanded by any correct scientific research.

Who, then, would dare to deny that all these labors can be set in motion by the desire really to learn what this passage actually says and what is meant by it? Who could gainsay that this motive springs from, or at any rate *could* spring from, reverence for the statements of Holy Scripture? It is therefore possible that the motive at work here may be the exact opposite of that which was operative in the destructive criticism of many rationalists. Whereas the latter pursued their critical reduction in order to gain a victory for the alleged truth of reason and therefore their own presuppositions, the practice today is to begin with *distrust* of one's own presuppositions. The fear is that one may have read certain traditional opinions, ideas that are, as it were, in the air around us, *into* the Bible and thus one is no longer a completely unbiased hearer. Now the conviction is that this secret tendency to assert and find confirmation for our own views is inconsistent with respect to the Word of God. The concern is therefore to break out of the prison of our own preconceived ideas and let the Scriptures themselves speak.

The church of Christ would be exceedingly ill-advised and would bring down upon itself the reproach of conservative self-righteousness of it denied to this endeavor its respect and then also its trust.

The fact that these endeavors often miscarry, that even this species of scholars bring with them *their* presuppositions—romantic or existentialistic—and apply them to the text, that they too become the victims of their own way of putting the question and the prejudice this can create—this is another question which can be discussed by itself. It shows us that even our thought processes remain in need of forgiveness and that they are performed in the shadow of the Fall.

Dialogue with our contemporaries and the succeeding generations is necessary to theology in order that we may become mutually aware of the blind spots in our eyes. Even though we ourselves have a beam in our eye, it may still be good to make our brother aware of the mote in *his* eye, for what we do not see in ourselves we recognize in others. The Lord had no intention whatsoever of forbidding us to do this. He only forbids the judging spirit in which as a rule it takes place.

Along with this readiness to take the statements of Scripture seriously there is still another and similar impulse of historical-critical study of the Bible. The scholar says to himself something like this: The texts we are listening to here are very ancient. They employ concepts and presuppositions which are different from

.ours. It would be wrong for us to take over these concepts and presuppositions (for example, the already mentioned cosmology in whose framework the statements of the creation story are made). This would be to confuse the *means* of the statement with the *intention* of the statement and therefore to misunderstand the text. We would be quite wrongly demanding too much of our faith. We would be obliged forcibly to repress something about which we know better. (For certainly it would be sad if in several thousand years we had learned nothing new about the "things of this world.") To do this would be to refuse to allow the message of the Word of God to search us out where we live here and now, but would rather be forcibly and falsely transporting ourselves into the past. How, then, could we go on preaching? For, after all, preaching means to allow the eternal Word to be heard as an actual reality here and now, to make it understood as something that is addressed to *me*. Therefore we have to speak it *afresh*, in the framework of our presuppositions, our cosmology, and our concepts. This, after all, is the reason why we do not simply recite the biblical texts from our pulpits, but rather expound them, grasp the burning torch of the witnesses and carry it right into our day, where it should burn and shine until it is taken up afresh by the next generation and carried further.

In order to do this we must very carefully work out the differences between the "then" (in which the text was written) and the "now" (in which it is to be heard). The more carefully this is done, the more realistically the work of proclaiming it as a present reality will be done and the more honest will be the appropriation of it. And, after all, this and nothing else is our concern. To express it somewhat more pointedly, we should not be estranged and led away from our own day by texts that come from a distant past; we should rather appropriate and make our own what is strange and far away.

Here I should like again to use Bultmann as an illustration, but only in the sense that he may be representative of many other theologians who are concerned with a historical-critical understanding of the Bible. When I am interested in the sources not merely as historical documents but rather study them in order to learn to understand something and allow them to become meaningful and important to me, there are really two tasks that belong together. The first is that I must inquire what the text meant in *its* historical setting and in the mouth of the author. This I can arrive at only by learning—among other things!—to differentiate the intention of the statement from the means of expression which are conditioned by the time and the situation in which it was uttered. (This is naturally a rather rough simplification of the task to be performed, but it may be sufficient to indicate the point I wish to make.)

But then the person who wants to understand is immediately confronted with the second task. If the message of the text is to be appropriated, he must also learn to know the person to whom he is to communicate it; he must also see *his* presuppositions and *his* questions. How can he present, for example, what Paul says about sin to someone for whom the question of guilt is not a real problem at all, who may be troubled by altogether different problems, for example, the fact that life passes so quickly, that he does not want to grow old and therefore holds on to his youth in an unnatural way, and therefore suffers because of his finitude? He may perhaps be asking all the wrong questions and thus missing the real point. But these are *his* questions and this is where I have to begin with my message. If I pay no attention whatever to the task of letting my message begin with the questions which are being asked and give answers only to questions which are not being asked, I shall hardly be successful in making it clear that what I have to say is real and urgent here and now.

It may be that the secret question of my hearer is *anxiety*, or loneliness, or boredom. It would be quite wrong to think that the gospel should have a simple, direct answer to all these questions; on the contrary, it will frequently have to *change* the way, the direction, in which the question is asked. But I only block the chance of this change taking place if I as the preacher do not face these questions and thus become aware of them.

Or how shall I speak about heaven if most people are naïve enough to think that heaven is the region where our astronauts travel? Here I certainly must do some translating in view of our changed conceptions. Otherwise the man of today who is so convinced of his modernity may suspect that in preaching my message about heaven I am trying to impose upon him an ancient or medieval cosmology.

In order, therefore, to translate the "then" into the "now" and become an interpreter of the text, I must really *know* the "then" and the "now." One of the available means of knowing the "then" can be the historical-critical study of the Bible.

But how do I learn to know the "now," my own time? In the first place, simply by being a contemporary person myself and therefore one who is touched and moved by the "now." The more vitally a person lives in his own time, the less he isolates himself, and the more he associates with people, observing what stirs them in their popular songs, television, and their literature, the more we may hope that he is feeling the pulsebeat of his time. But he who wants to go beyond this, as a theologian certainly should, and subject his knowledge to the strict discipline of definition will also consult philosophy, which is a form of reflection upon the contemporary mind (at all events, in addition of other things it is this *also*), to find out what it has to say about the fundamental questions of present-day existence.

This is exactly what Bultmann is trying to do when he takes Heidegger's philosophy as a model from which the modern mind can be read and proceeds on the basis of this philosophy to question the New Testament and then seeks to incorporate its answers into the scheme of this philosophy. The ordinary Christian who becomes acquainted with statements of this kind is often shocked by the diction which is so alien to the Bible (terms such as self-understanding, *Selbstverständnis*, being-ready-to-hand, *Zuhandenheit*, etc.). Quite frankly, I do not care for it much myself, nor has it by any means become more attractive to me through my having learned how to handle it. But this is not the point at all. The non-biblical terminology, which one also finds coming out of Tillich's virtuosity in word coinage, can be a sign that here is one who is engaged in an act of radical contemporization, uncompromisingly carrying out the task of translation which we have discussed. If this is so, then it would be a sign of the intensity of the will to understand and to appropriate the message. And I have no doubt that these theologians have exactly this intention.

Therefore this is not the point where the critical counterquestions begin at all; they enter in at an entirely different level. Perhaps the important critical question might be formulated as follows: Is it not conceivable that the modern mind may turn out to be not only the "place" to which one wishes to bring the message but at the same time the "norm" for what we think we can accept in this message and what we think we can allow to be of "concern" to us? May it not be possible that just because we know what the modern mind is, we may have already made up our minds as to what the Word of God can be for us? Could not, therefore, the questions that are put by the modern mind be already prejudicing the possible answers contained in the kerygma, and is it not conceivable that I am no longer capable of hearing something utterly new, something that simply bowls me over and goes beyond my questions?

I am not concerned, however, at the moment with a critical discussion of this point. I mention it here lest anybody think that my only purpose is to be an uncritical advocate of historical criticism. What I am really concerned about is that you gain a little appreciation of the positive motive behind the historical-critical study of the Bible, of its intention to understand and (honestly) appropriate the Scriptures.

QUESTION: I believe that we are now in the clear about this motive. But what good does it do us if it is only a matter of motive? You yourself have pointed out that this alleged appropriation can turn out to be something like "swallowing" the message and that then one may possibly be worse off than before when one simply allowed the texts to stand in all their greatness without manipulating them with this honest intention of "understanding" it. Instead, they are now being manipulated to death. At any rate, this is often the impression I have. Quite frankly, I still count myself among those who are a little afraid to enter this whole field. You never know in whose hands you will fall. You may not be spiritually curried, but only fleeced! And the very thing you took up for the sake of your faith may lead to your losing your faith altogether.

ANSWER: Don't you ever enjoy an adventure? Pascal once said that it is a glorious thing to be on a ship when you know for sure that it will reach the harbor. We do know that it will—or don't we? Why then shouldn't we let the wind whistle about our ears? If anybody here is too timid, too concerned about his fundamentalist security, I would like to answer him in the form of a parable.

Not a few of my fundamentalist brethren, whom I seek in honest love and certainly not in pharisaic pride, remind me of the disciples on the ship crossing the Sea of Galilee with the Lord on board. There they are by themselves—for, of course, the Lord is sleeping—prowling about the ship, listening to the creaking in the ship's sides and peering from the railings into the water to see whether they can discover some Bult- or frogman down there boring a hole in the ship's side. When the Lord finally woke up, to his amazement he saw his men aimlessly and excitedly running about instead of being at their nautical stations, performing their regular duties, while the ship had obviously gotten off course. Then he asked them, "Why aren't you paying attention to the course instead of running about as you are?" They answered, "We're looking out to see whether some Bult- or frogman is boring into our ship." And the Lord said, "Why should that interest you?" The disciples replied, "But, dear Lord, how can you ask such a thing? If the ship gets a hole in it, the water will come in!" And the Lord said, "Yes, and what then?" The disciples said, "Why, the ship will go down." Whereupon the Lord said, "So that's what you are afraid of! O men of little faith, don't you know that the ship can never go down as long as I am sleeping in it, as long as I am with you?"

As I said, this is often the way my fundamentalist friends strike me when they worry about the ship of Holy Scripture possibly going down, even though the Lord is in it.

We should not worry about the ship at all, but rather perform our regular duties on it. This would be the kind of relativism that would befit the children of God.

Perhaps in conclusion I may venture to sum it up rather boldly in this way. (But this often serves to make things clear. And anybody who has not understood me by this time is likely to choke on it anyhow.) I am not primarily interested in the Bible at all. I am interested only in the Lord Jesus Christ. The Holy Scripture is only the ship in which he sleeps. And because *he* is sleeping in it, I am *then* also interested in the ship. May it not be that many of the questionable theses of the Fundamentalists derive from the fact that they have reversed this order of interest? And would it not be well if they would first get into the clear about this order of priority in faith?

QUESTION: May I, despite the lateness of the hour, ask one last question? I think it can be answered briefly. [The audience approved.] Do I understand you aright when I conclude that you therefore do not think of the historical criticism of the Bible as being something that we are "caught with," something that "fatefully" comes down upon us to make our faith more difficult? Do you believe that this method of investigation is rather an *enrichment* of theology?

ANSWER: Especially with regard to those who always think they see in this a threat to their faith (and who do this the more, the less they set themselves to this task), one could reply with the Scripture passage: "We know that in everything God works for good with those who love him."[4] Now you certainly will not take the citation of that passage as a kind of pious, comforting

---

[4] Rom. 8:28.

reassurance. I use it rather to point to a very sober fact, and that is that everything depends on the intention with which I pursue the critical study of the Bible. I attempted to set forth the two basic intentions which are possible here: *first*, the rationalistic (or better, pseudo-rationalistic) goal of self-confirmation engaged in by the rational man who must therefore aim to demolish "historical authorities," and *second*, the opposite goal which is to allow the Scriptures to speak for themselves, to take seriously the entrance of God into history, to get rid of one's own preconceptions, to see clearly the interval of time between the "then" and the "now," and in all this to seek devotedly and self-forgetfully to "understand."

One may say that only the *latter* attitude toward the Holy Scriptures is worthy of "those who love God." But then it is also easy to see how this intention "works for the good" of their inquiring and their will to understand. In this way they get down to the oneness of the biblical witness. But this oneness is then no longer —as in the doctrine of verbal inspiration, which puts all the statements of the Bible on the same level—a unity of sameness and uniformity, but rather of diversity. By distinguishing between the individual sources of the Pentateuch, for example, one discovers a new diversity of emphases and points of view. The determination of varying historical situations and circumstances show what a great breadth of variation there is in the way in which God speaks to men and the way men react to this speech of God in their witness.

This can be seen very clearly—to mention only one example— in the relation of the Pauline writings to the Epistle of James. There is a difference of situation between the two documents and therefore a shift in the way the theological question is stated. Paul had already foreseen the possible danger of a misunderstanding which might lurk in his proclamation of the sole effectuality of grace, namely, that it could be used as a pillow to rest upon and thus result in an indifference toward sin. After all, if everything depends on grace, then we can simply continue as before, then nothing can separate us from God. On the contrary, the deeper we descend into sin the greater chance we give to grace to demonstrate its sole effectuality.[5] This would surely be a misunderstanding of his message. And the fact is that it promptly gained ground. And it is to this situation that the Epistle of James addresses itself when it admonishes us to be doers of the Word, and not hearers only.[6] This sounds (and many exegetes have so interpreted it) as if the author of the Epistle of James meant to formulate a kind of antithesis to Paul's teaching and reintroduce work righteousness. In reality, however, something quite different appears to be the case. Paul brought the first breakthrough to a new understanding of Law and Gospel. But James addresses himself to those who, though they understood that the Law had been overcome, had nevertheless misunderstood this overcoming grace itself and were turning it into a kind of principle of indifference. This meant that they had not understood the overcoming of the Law after all and thus found themselves not, as they should have, in the liberty of the children of God, but rather in libertinism.

If we take the theses of Paul and James by themselves in isolation, they appear to contradict each other. But if we see them in their historical relationship to each other and if we discern the point of the message which they both have in view, they complement each other as witnesses of the same testimony. What is different in them arises from the situation of the people to whom they are addressed. To be sure, only he can see this who not only keeps in view the point of comparison but also stands in an existential relationship to it. (This is one place, I think, where the much overworked word "existential" can really be used.) But then the diversity of the testimonies has the effect of a piece of color printing whose various layers of color unite to form an impressively colorful picture. And the tension between Paul and James has gradually become the classical model of the tension to

[5] Cf. Rom. 6:1-15.
[6] Jas. 1:22; 2:17.

which all faith in the sole effectuality of grace is exposed (in every church and in every individual) and for the overcoming of which it needs "admonition" and correction.

So here we not only stand beneath a "cloud" of witnesses[7] but we also have before us a many-voiced "choir" of witnesses. But the very richness of this polyphony becomes apparent to us only when we cease thinking of the Bible as a book that fell "finished" from heaven, but rather see it as the historical documentation of a history with God, far more delicately graduated in tone and color and with far more levels and strata than even the most attentive Bible reader can discover by himself.

Thus the historical, depth-perspective with which we read the Scriptures now, the clearer knowledge we have of sources and redactions, actually give us a picture of the testimony which is far more colorful and polyphonic than was ever suspected before. We hear the people of God praising the mighty acts of God in the richest variety of tongues.[8] And for the believer the oneness of the witness only becomes greater and clearer as it comes to him in the diversity of witnesses and thus makes itself something to be searched and sought for.

If a more rigorously theological formulation of this is desired, I would put it this way: Ontologically (which means here, objectively), the unity of the kerygma is antecedent to the diversity of its witness. But noetically (which means here, in the way this becomes apparent to our cognition) we must first *search for* this unity behind the frequently confusing historical diversity, behind the very lively chorus of voices. But, of course, even this is not altogether correct, for all theory (and the historical-critical investigation of the Bible is, after all, something theoretical!) is *preceded* by the pretheoretical structure of faith! Before we take the philological plummet and the historical telescope in hand, we have already *heard* the message of the Scriptures, and the news of the God of Abraham, Isaac, and Jacob—who is the Father of

[7] Heb. 12:1.
[8] Acts 2:11.

Jesus Christ—has already overtaken us. And because it is the one
God whose Word joins the diversified whole of the Scriptures into
a unity, we too are met first by this unity. Only then do we
penetrate, in a secondary act of theoretical endeavor, to the
diversity and finally regain the unity in a deeper and richer form.

In this process—which again is itself a part of our history with
God!—we may have to pass through stages in which we lose
sight of this unity and everything seems to fall apart from the
explosive power of the historical. And there have been many
whose faith has suffered shipwreck and who have not endured
the hazards of this search for truth—at least as far as the limited
sight of human eyes can see. I mention this expressly because I
do not want to make it appear that I am here recommending
the historical-critical investigation of the Scriptures as a method
of spiritual discipline which will necessarily lead a person by
logical and absolutely sure steps to the fullness of faith. There are
no such methods anywhere else in the spiritual life, nor is there
one here. There is no point in the spiritual life nor any movement
which creates this spiritual life in the realm of theory at which
we are not dependent upon the grace of the Holy Spirit.

Therefore even the most learned theologian, the most expert
examiner of the sources, and the most erudite biblical historian
never gets beyond the state of the "poor in spirit." Our works
do not justify us and our scholarly works do not bring us nearer
to God. Here too it all depends, not on our searching and seeking,
but on God's mercy. Our feet may slip and stumble either way—
through craving for knowledge and through the repression of
knowledge. Our deliverance lies in him who opens our deaf ears
and blind eyes that we may see him at the vanishing point of every
biblical perspective. In this sense we are always setting out toward
someone who has already overtaken us and from whom we came
in the first place. For, as Augustine said, we would not be able
to seek him if he had not already found us.

III

Understanding the Bible

THE NATURE AND IMPORTANCE OF HERMENEUTICS

QUESTION: If you approve of the historical-critical study of the Bible, then obviously you also ally yourself with the hermeneutical endeavors which perhaps constitute the greatest part of theological discussion today. Is this supposition correct?

ANSWER: In order to answer that question, I would suggest that we examine for a moment the term "hermeneutics." The word goes back to the Greek verb *hermeneuein* in which a whole bundle of meanings are brought together. The meaning that finally prevailed, however, was that of "understanding something" or "making something understood." As an expression for the "art of understanding" the term appears first in Plato.[1] It occurs in this form in the New Testament only once, in Luke,[2] where it means to expound or interpret the Scriptures. In the usual signification of the term as a discipline of understanding it was not used until very late, probably not before the seventeenth century.[3] The most famous hermeneutics of modern time we owe to Friedrich Schleiermacher. He begins with the simple "hermeneutical" fact that our speech is a means of mutual understanding and that all understanding presupposes a definite relation "between the speaker

---

[1] *hermèneutiké techné*. [For an illuminating, almost exhausting assembly of the etymology of this term and its derivatives see the discussion by James M. Robinson in *The New Hermeneutic* (New York: Harper & Row, 1964), pp. 1 ff. Trans.]

[2] Luke 24:27.

[3] Here it occurs in the title of the work of the Orthodox theologian J. C. Dannhauer, *Hermeneutica sacra sive methodus exponendarum sacrarum litterarum*, 1654.

and the hearer." Later Wilhelm Dilthey, following Schleier-macher's lead, said that only analogues can understand each other, or, to put it another way, one can understand only that which is "already contained in the living apprehending being." Conse-quently, I could never comprehend what Plato or Paul say about justice if I did not already have within me the question of justice and a preunderstanding of what it can be.

This is precisely the point where the question whether there can be such a thing as a hermeneutics at all in theology enters in. Are we in a relationship of analogy to God and his Word, to "revela-tion"? Is not God rather the "Wholly Other," the very one whom we *cannot* understand and who therefore must disclose, "reveal" himself to us? Is this not also the reason why Paul speaks of "what no eye has seen, nor ear heard, nor the heart of man conceived?"[4] What then is the use of an art of understanding? If the "Wholly Other" is without analogy, then it is in principle incomprehensible and any hermeneutical endeavor whatsoever would be a kind of illegitimate usurpation.

In this connection it is interesting to note that Paul is obviously aware of this hermeneutical problem, or better, this goal of human hermeneutics. In I Corinthians 2:11 he addresses himself directly to the fact that if there is to be understanding there must be an analogy between the speaker and the hearer. There he says: "What person knows a man's thoughts except the spirit of the man which is in him? So also no one comprehends the thoughts of God except the Spirit of God." What this means is that only a man is analogous to himself. Therefore only a human being (and not a dog, say, however smart he may be) can understand another human being. But for the same reason this human being *cannot* understand God. He is not analogous to him.

In order to proceed here, we must consider for a moment *why* man is not analogous to God. If man is created in the image of God, this assumes a certain degree of analogy; for after all, the image is *like* him who is imaged in it. And, though we cannot

[4] I Cor. 2:9.

here develop the substantiating argument,[5] we may also say that man does not *lose* this character of being God's image, but that it is rather indestructible.

Now, man's nonanalogousness certainly does not consist (at least not primarily) in the fact that the human mind is too small and too mean to think God's "higher thoughts."[6] It is not differences of degree that matter here. The decisive thing that breaks the analogy lies rather in the fact that man in his *existence* turns away from God, that he refuses to be a creature and a child of God and wants to be his own lord.[7] He thereby becomes turned in upon himself (*incurvatus in se*, as Luther puts it). The relationship to God which he thus disclaims even then remains constitutive of his existence; he never loses it; but now it acquires features which are in the strict sense "perverse." Instead of humbly acknowledging his creatureliness, he proceeds to *create* his own gods. Hence that which puts him in the state of nonalogousness and inadequacy and thus deprives him of the basis for understanding is an attitude of his whole existence and not merely a too constricted radius of action on the part of his mind or reason. He who wants himself cannot want God. And he who on principle does not want God also cannot understand him. His ears hear nothing, his eyes see nothing, and nothing comes into his heart. On this level of existence hermeneutical endeavors are completely fruitless. And yet that saying which speaks of blind eyes, deaf ears, and locked and barred hearts has a continuation. It says that God has revealed what has not been heard (and cannot be heard) and what has not been seen (and cannot be seen) to those who love him, because he has brought them out of that state of being turned in upon themselves. On this new plane which God has established, the whole question of understanding may therefore look quite different. But how are we to think of it?

It will be best if we consider once more that saying of Paul in

---

[5] Cf. the section on the *imago Dei* in *Theologische Ethik*, Vol. I, pp. 267 ff.
[6] Isa. 55: 8-9.
[7] Rom. 1:21.

I Corinthians 2:11. There it is said that only God knows what is in God. (Man therefore does not know this, at any rate not in his introverted state.) Now we also know how to account for this remarkable statement of Paul: There is no being that is analogous to God. Therefore no being can understand him. Only God is analogous to himself. Therefore only he, and he alone, can understand himself. God's truth is solely in his self-consciousness.

Therefore if there is to be such a thing as theological knowledge, an understanding of the Word and the mighty acts of God, then the analogy to God which men have given up must be restored in a new act of creation. The divine Word must create its own hearers. (For there are no longer any hearers who would understand it "naturally.") The theological locus in which this creative function of the Word—or if you will—this "creation of the hearer," is dealt with is the doctrine of the Holy Spirit. For this doctrine declares that we are called to share in God's self-knowledge and thus to be put into the proper analogy. The Holy Spirit, who enlightens us, is none other than God himself. In him and through him we become partakers of that which God himself knows about himself. For the Spirit (not man's reason, but *this* Spirit, the *Holy* Spirit) "searches everything, even the depths of God."[8]

This passage also makes it clear why theology can never allow its processes of acquiring knowledge to be accused of being "heteronomous." Heteronomy would be present only if the object of faith and thus also the knowledge of it were dictated from the outside and hence if there were actually such things as dogmas in the sense of "compulsory articles of faith." But for him who has been called into the new analogy there is no such dictation, but only a free spontaneity of faith. This faith—like love—is not commanded, dictated to him, but rather won from him through the superior power of what happens to him. That which for faith is spontaneity is for the act of cognition, which is co-ordinated

8 I Cor. 2:10.

with faith, "evidence." But since this evidence is not disposable, theological statements can never have the character of demonstrations or proofs, but only the character of proclamation, address, appeal.

On this basis, then, there certainly is such a thing as a theological hermeneutics. The believer's attitude to that which he believes is one of open *readiness* to understand. He knows that he has been transposed into a new conformity with God and that he wills what God wills (or prays that he may so will). Thus he interprets what is reported to him about the words and the mighty acts of God from the point of view of that *heart* of God which he trusts and which reveals and manifests itself in these words and acts.

In this sense every sermon is an effort to make the Word of God understood. This concern is expressed even in the very fact that the sermon expounds a text of Holy Scripture and in this exposition shows that it is seeking to help people to appropriate it with understanding. It therefore calls the text out of the "then" when it was written into the "now" in which it is heard and is intended to meet and speak to the hearer.

But there can be no mistaking of the fact that the "spiritual" hermeneutics which is operative here is fundamentally different from the formally parallel exegesis of *other* texts—such as the writings of Plato, for example. For spiritual hermeneutics, and thus the exposition of Holy Scriptures which takes place in preaching, can be carried out only with an ultimate humble reservation, namely, the realization that the expositor himself *cannot* bring about the sought-for understanding and that here as everywhere else the exposition (understood as human "work") is powerless. For the expositor does not have it in his power to create the conditions under which understanding and appropriation are possible at all. For, after all, these conditions consist in the hearer's having been *called* into the new being, into a new conformity with God. This, after all, is the only way in which an end is put to the condition in which he sees but does not perceive and hears but does not understand.[9] This miracle only the Holy Spirit can perform through the Word which creates its own hearers.

Thus understanding is dependent on conditions for which the preacher can only pray, but which he can neither presuppose nor produce by means of his own persuasive power. This is why the pulpit prayer is essential to the sermon. And we know the great emphasis which the liturgical pulpit prayers put upon this powerlessness of the preacher to produce these conditions of understanding and therefore upon the coming and the aid of the Holy Spirit.

QUESTION: Is what you have defined as the basis of a "spiritual hermeneutics" also taken into account in Bultmann's position? I have the impression that he simply regards the kerygma as being understandable in the general sense, provided that one applies the right hermeneutical principles. But these can be understood. In other words, one can be brought (or shall I say, one can be compelled) to hear the kerygma's call to decision. Here it would seem to me that there is no room left for Jesus' statement that the natural man can see but not perceive and hear but not understand. And correspondingly, there also seems to be not much room for the miracle of the Holy Spirit.

ANSWER: I would think that we could not be too careful about making such judgments. It would be of great interest and importance to hear Bultmann himself speak to this question. It is possible that in that case one would be obliged—as always when one goes to the bottom of a theology—to distinguish between the faith and the teaching of a theologian. I would never dare to assert that a man like Bultmann fundamentally disputes the fact declared in Mark 4:12, namely, that man cannot control the existential conditions for understanding. And likewise I would also not dare to say that he denies the significance of the miracle of the

[9] Mark 4:12.

Spirit in the process of understanding. It is another question, however, whether all this has an adequate place in the system of his thought and therefore whether the theological *author* can provide an adequate thought structure for that which to the believing Christian is certain (and perhaps self-evident).

This question arises not only with respect to Bultmann but with respect to all of us, that is to say, anybody who attempts to do any independent theological thinking. We must always keep in mind that our faith is greater than our theology. (There are, of course, pathological forms of theological existence in which theology is greater than faith, that is, where one teaches theologically more than one can defend on the basis of one's personal faith. But we cannot discuss this here.) With these reservations and therefore with due caution I can accept the question which has been asked and speak to it. In this case I can do this with less restraint since I think I can conclude that my questioner has read these works himself and reflected upon them.

I too have the impression that it is at least an open *question* whether Bultmann proceeds in the sense of the spiritual hermeneutics which I have sketched, whether he therefore gives due place and value to the miracle of the Spirit. Again and again it strikes me that Bultmann's approach assumes that there is an all too smooth transition from the self-understanding of man *before* faith to the self-understanding of man *in* faith, a transition which, basically, can be made by "anyone" (and therefore also by the natural man). He speaks, for example, of a "pre-understanding" of the natural man in which he shows certain attitudes toward his finitude, the future, guilt, and also toward God. In the encounter with the kerygma this pre-understanding is, so to speak, "overtaken" and reshaped into the transformed and new self-understanding of the believer. So regarded, it would in principle still be possible to explain the new self-understanding of the believer as something beyond man's control and accordingly to interpret the believing understanding of the kerygma as an event which is given by the Spirit and cannot be grasped by one's own unaided power.

This interpretation, it seems to me, would be possible in principle since, after all, the kerygma accomplishes in me a *change* of self-understanding, because it constitutes a kind of intervention which overmasters me and which I do not "choose" by my own decision. Thus there would be a clear break between existence *before* faith and existence *in* faith. It would be unjust to Bultmann not to state this with all clarity.

And yet, as I said, it seems to me to be true[10] that certain principles of Bultmann's hermeneutics prevent one from availing oneself of this altogether inherent possibility. Let me substantiate this briefly.

The pre-understanding with which the natural man approaches the kerygma by no means signifies merely a precedency in time. It is therefore not merely of historical and biographical interest because it may contain something like a description of the state of a man's mind *before* faith. Rather this pre-understanding signifies far more than that. It also has a normative, prejudicating, prejudicing significance. I quote only one statement which shows this very emphatically: *"The understanding of records about events as the action of God presupposes a pre-understanding of what the action of God as such can mean."*[11] The pre-understanding therefore pegs out in a prejudicial way the boundaries within which any serious summons to regard something as the action of God can reach me at all. Expressed somewhat crudely, one cannot expect "everything" from me. I possess certain principles of selection which filter the great mass of records and separate the acceptable from the unacceptable.

For example, my pre-understanding makes it entirely clear to

---

[10] I have endeavored on other occasions to establish this more fully, for example in "Reflections on Bultmann's Hermeneutic," *The Expository Times*, LXVII (1956), pp. 154-157, 175-177, and in *The Easter Message Today, Three Essays* by Leonhard Goppelt, Helmut Thielicke, and Hans-Rudolf Muller-Schwefe (New York: Thomas Nelson & Sons, 1964), pp. 59-116.

[11] *Zeitschrift für Theologie und Kirche*, 47, 1950, p. 66. [Cf. English translation in "The Problem of Hermeneutics," *Essays, Philosophical and Theological*, tr. by James C. G. Greig (New York: The Macmillan Company, 1955), p. 257.]

me that the action of God cannot be "objectively manifest" ("*gegenständlich vorfindlich*"), that it cannot meet me as an extraordinary act, say, as a *miracle* which projects beyond the ordinary course of events. For my pre-understanding is after all the self-understanding of a modern man who in the sciences rigidly relies upon "self-sufficient immanence" and the closed economy of natural forces. Certain ways of divine action which are communicated to me in the Bible—I am referring to such extraordinary action as, for example, the resurrection of Jesus on the third day—therefore never come into my purview at all as possible objects of my understanding—at any rate not in so far as I could reckon with them as real facts. My "pre-given" principles of selection simply eliminate them. But then this makes the facticity of the revelatory event highly questionable.

Naturally, Bultmann not only *knows* this; he says it expressly. This comes out, for example, in his understanding of the resurrection accounts. For him the resurrection is not a fact,[12] but rather a commentary on the cross of Jesus, a mythological code word for the interpretation of the meaning of his death. But this loss of facticity plays no role whatsoever in Bultmann's thinking. For the kerygma produces only the change in my self-understanding, it produces an event in my *consciousness*. Moreover, my faith relates only to this "event," and only this "event" is the hermeneutical principle by which I interpret the kerygma. But then the problem of facticity no longer plays any role; for the inbreaking of an event into my consciousness does not need to happen under the pressure of a factual event (such as an earthquake, a catastrophic situation, or an exalting event). This inbreaking can come from a text, from the performance of a play, or from reading Plato. This too can "upset," shock, and change my previous self-understanding.

[12] I pass over here the question, again discussed elsewhere, whether such a fact—if one really accepts it as a saving "event"—lies on the same level with the historical events of Jesus' life (e.g., the cross) or whether it is beyond having ontological quality and thus also removed from normal historical perception.

We see therefore how normative and prejudicial the pre-understanding can actually be and how it determines in advance what can claim and what cannot claim to be understood as the action of God. Thus there can be no really serious break when the threshold of faith is crossed, at any rate no break that would be essentially different from the break which other encounters in this world can effect in me.

The analogy between pre-understanding and the self-understanding of faith thus appears to be complete and unbroken. It comes about by way of faith in a process of understanding, the individual phases of which are seamlessly joined together. Accordingly, there seems to me to be no place here for the assertion that the Word "creates" its own hearers, that is, that the analogy is established in the uncontrollable miracle of the Spirit, that it is *given* to me as a new existence in conformity with God. It really seems to me that what we have here is something like an "uprising of the hermeneutical means" and that what was meant merely to help me to understand becomes determinative; it dictates altogether what the object of my understanding is to be. But when that happens, then it would appear to me that hermeneutics loses its spiritual character: it is no longer an aid to the perception of a claim, but rather makes its own claims.

It would seem to me that this latent transformation of the hermeneutical functions is already heralded in Bultmann's insistent advocacy of the term "hermeneutical principle." He means by this the point of view from which I interrogate the kerygma in order that as I pursue this interrogation I may understand it. This point of view consists, as we saw, in the change of one's self-understanding and thus in the "overtaking" of one's pre-understanding. And I believe that I have shown, however briefly, that this point of view constitutes a contraction, a pre-selection.

For me this observation by itself makes the term "hermeneutical principle" dubious. More accurately, I reject it. The term "principle" expresses the timeless neutral state of a point of view. And this is precisely what cannot be. There is no standpoint, no point of view "outside," which can remain untouched and unmodified in the history of faith. There is no discernible schema within which this history occurs continuously (because it is held together by this schema).

This, naturally, does not mean that I would deny every kind of question, pre-understanding, and bent of interpretation with which one approaches the kerygma. To deny this would be sheer nonsense. I cannot obliterate myself as a living person and turn myself into an unsubstantial vacuum which is prepared in indifferent passivity to absorb "everything." The very fact that I approach the kerygma with the willingness to pursue the question of truth shows that I am no longer a *tabula rasa*, but rather that I am critical. I may perhaps be willing to allow my pre-understanding to be overcome and to undertake revisions (the extent to which I can actually do this of myself is another question), but I am never simply "empty" and open to "everything." This, after all, would make me completely defenseless over against the profession of things that claim to be the truth and the existential appeals which I encounter, creating an utterly absurd situation. *Naturally*, I have my expectations, criteria, and questions. *Naturally*, I peg out in my mind the boundaries within which I am willing to allow someone to talk to me about an act of God. But can these "pre-given" factors in my consciousness really be called "principles"?

I would say that this dubious term, which goes hand in hand with timelessness, would be permissible only on *one* condition, that is, if we were to speak of "heuristic" principles. By this we mean provisional assumptions. They are also called hypotheses. They play their part, for example, in scientific experiments. There an experimental procedure is set up on the assumption that such and such biological or physical facts are true and observations are made as to how nature reacts to this assumption. It can either confirm or disprove the assumption. If it is confirmed, the hypothesis results in an assured proposition. If it is disproved, the hypothesis is abandoned.

The heuristic principle, as it is illustrated by the hypothesis, is therefore a provisional assumption, as it were, an interim principle. It is true that I apply it to nature as a principle of understanding.[13] I am prepared, however, in the next moment to have it shattered by this very nature and allow myself to be compelled to make revisions. I am willing to have my question and the principles that underlie it be overtaken by the counterquestion of nature. This expresses the provisional character of the heuristic principle.

I would say, then, that only in this sense could there be anything like a "hermeneutical principle." No man can say in advance what happens or may happen to him in the encounter with the gospel. At any rate, in the pastoral dialogues of Jesus (which we have discussed in other connections) the replies of Jesus are never on the same level with the previous questions men put to him. The gospel can contain some rude surprises with regard to what we may consider true and possible *after* meeting with him. It can change the whole context of what I have hitherto regarded as real. It can really create in me a new hearer who must leave behind all the ideas about what can be heard and understood, which he formerly clung to. Then, too, hermeneutics may be placed upon an entirely new footing. And then, if one still has left any desire to talk about hermeneutical principles, they may possibly look totally different from what one thought before.

The fact is that we can see this breakdown of our preconceived principles taking place in other areas. Naturally, I can hear and therefore seek to understand the commandments of God only because I have a moral consciousness and am prepared to listen to the claims of duty. Now it is very interesting to observe what happens in the encounter with the commandments of God—say in their radicalized form in the Sermon on the Mount.

Since Kant has defined the moral consciousness in such classical form, as perhaps no one else has done so well, his concept of the

[13] The term "to understand" is not altogether correct in the context of natural science since it relates to personal life and therefore describes a humanistic category. We use it here *cum grano salis* because we wish to bring out the analogy to theological hermeneutics.

"practical reason" can here serve as a model. Kant says that the moral commandment that sounds in my conscience is obligatory because it at the same time bestows upon me the consciousness of freedom. I can feel seriously obligated only when I know that I am obligated within the bonds of my *ability*. If someone demands of me something utterly impossible (asserting, for example, that it is my duty to fly to Venus), this is *not* an obligation to be taken seriously. It simply fizzles out without touching my conscience. Thus Kant arrives at the axiom: "You can because you ought."

Now with a moral consciousness so structured I listen to the claim of the Sermon on the Mount, the demand that I must not anger my brother, for example, or the statement that it is contrary to the will of God to "look at a woman lustfully." I am thus confronted with the fact that God makes a total claim upon me, not merely within the possible latitude of my *actions*, but in my whole *being*. He makes this claim upon me because I came forth intact from his hands and he can demand that I give myself back to him in the same state.[14] But my being is not at my disposal. I cannot make myself different from what I am, or better, from what I have *become*. I can to some extent control my actions, but not the plane of being on which my actions are enacted. And it is precisely this plane of being that Christ puts in question when he makes his radical demands.

The consequence is that I must confess: "I ought but I cannot." For Kant's doctrine of moral principle this is an utterly absurd statement, since for him this fundamental nonability does away with moral obligation. It is actually an indication that it was not a genuine "ought" at all.

Thus we are confronted with an extremely remarkable phenomenon. I encounter the commandments of God with my moral consciousness. I can hear them only as a human being. An animal or a stone cannot do this. The human element in me which enables me to perceive in this way is exactly this moral consciousness; it

[14] Cf. the chapter on "creation from nothing" (*creatio ex nihilo*) in *Theologische Ethik*, Vol. I.

is my conscience. But in the next moment this moral consciousness proves to be incapable of appropriating the content of the commandment. The Geiger counter of the conscience, which has just signaled that here there is present a moral "radiation," in the next moment flies out of my hands. The instrument of perception is shattered. The co-ordinating system into which I wanted to incorporate the relative moral value of the divine commandments is incapable of allowing this to be done. The assertion upon which the unconditional demands of the Sermon on the Mount rest (namely, that I came intact from the hands of God and must give myself back to him in the same state) constitutes a premise which is alien to the moral consciousness, which it cannot arrive at by itself, and therefore transcends its presuppositions.

Thus we find here a process of "overtaking" which is quite similar to that which we described in connection with the hermeneutical principle.

If I were to describe what happens here in "religious" language, I would say that no one leaves the encounter with the gospel as he was when he entered it. But this should be stated even more sharply. He not only leaves this encounter "changed," modified in his self-consciousness, but is translated to a completely new plane of being with a correspondingly new understanding of reality and history. He is not only "changed" but "created" anew, transposed as a "new creature" to a new plane of being. And because now he "is" different (in the ontological sense), everything now looks different to him (in the noetic sense). Therefore his hermeneutical conditions also are different.

And here I ask myself very seriously whether the deepest problem with Bultmann does not lie at this point. I hesitate to state it simply as a thesis and would prefer to put it in the form of a question: Is not this possibility of a "new creation" lacking in Bultmann's presentation? Is there nothing more here than "change" within the framework of the same schema of existence? And therefore is not the transition from Heidegger to Paul too smooth? Is there anything more here than mere variations on an identical plane? Is this perhaps the reason why it lacks a doctrine of the Holy Spirit (at any rate one that has pre-eminence)?

Every theology has to concern itself with the question of man as he is *before* his encounter with Christ, *before* faith. And anybody who does not get the answer to this question from the Old Testament must get it from philosophy. To co-ordinate the two would appear to be only conditionally possible. You have only to look at the history of theology to see illustrations of what looks almost like an alternative choice. Which of the two is "sound doctrine"? I can leave this question to your own reflection. But you will allow me to add this one comment. Even beginning this question with the Old Testament does not insure us against foolishness. The simple application of the formula "prophecy and fulfillment" could lead us right past the decisive point. A great deal of mischief has been done with it. But perhaps there is an objectively more justified form of beginning with the Old Testament (and then also with the relationship of "prophecy and fulfillment"). In this safeguarded sense, then, I ask: From where shall I obtain the "substructure" for the doctrine of our encounter with the kerygma, from the Old Testament or from Heidegger (or his colleagues)?

CONCLUDING QUESTION BY THE MODERATOR: I would like to hear more about the significance of the Old Testament, particularly in this respect, but I realize that this would require a great deal of time. Allow me instead to ask a more practical question. I also raise it partly out of human kindness, for the discussion so far has made considerable demands upon us. It was a German mode of thinking which is fond of the abstract. This does not imply any criticism, for when one devotes onself to such questions one must also think in abstract terms. And since we find ourselves here among teachers of theology, we need not be so afraid of this either.

But it is in this connection that we professors particularly have a very practical question to ask. If I understood you correctly, I take it that you would not be adverse to having our students, during their training, also engage in hermeneutical studies. You yourself have shown how thinking through hermeneutical questions can lead to some very central theological problems. Nevertheless I have certain pedagogical doubts about students concerning themselves too much with it. Yet I do not wish to state these doubts myself at this time, but would rather hear what you have to say about it. Perhaps I may be permitted to speak again later.

ANSWER: I too have such doubts and possibly they are similar to yours. These doubts do not relate to the fact that one should concern oneself with hermeneutics (naturally one should!), but only to the way in which it is so often done today. Indeed, something like a hermeneutical hullabaloo, a monomanic excess, has erupted among us. The hermeneutical circle threatens to become a circus. And I have noted with some concern that several theological faculties in Europe have even established special institutes for hermeneutics. I am not now saying anything against hermeneutics but only against the hypertrophy of hermeneutics. (Likewise, I have never yet said anything against liturgy, though I have protested against "liturgism.")

Hermeneutics does have in it a certain danger in so far as it readily exercises a fascination upon intelligent young people. For one thing, this fascination can be accounted for by the fact that it is an exceedingly interesting science. The process of understanding is a very elementary act of human life. And then, too, the subjects to which this analysis of understanding is applied (great literature or the Bible too) enter in and have their own attraction. So far so good. But here comes the hitch. As an intelligent young man I can very quickly join in with talk about hermeneutical questions. All you have to do is to pick up a few methodological and epistemological terms and tricks and, lo, you can talk along with the rest of them. When I think of a symposium of our great Old and New Testament scholars in which the theology of the Deuteronomist or of the Qumran texts are discussed, these theological mice and greenhorns (pardon me!) keep their mouths shut and become all ears. But when the same group of eminent men talk about the hermeneutical principle, these boys merrily join the chorus of their elders and there is no end to the chatter.

The point is that you can talk about hermeneutics even though you possess a minimum of material knowledge. Naturally, this chance is exceedingly attractive. During my rectorate at the University in Germany I often observed that the representatives of the student body were able to rattle off some highly ingenious statements about university reform, the tasks of university education and instruction, etc. Often they were able to do this at least as well as the old professors; for it is possible to talk about the nature of study without having studied onself. And what the old professors had arrived at on the basis of dealing with their subject and their vocation the "young sprouts" (again, pardon me) had already "doped out" with their own bright minds. But if what Nietzsche said about our not wanting to hear some truths "from toothless mouths" is right, then it is also true that there are many truths which we do not care to hear from mouths filled with milk teeth (for the third time, excuse me).

This applies exactly to hermeneutics. This question must arise from work on the texts themselves, but must not be placed before it, as if one must first settle this question before beginning to read the texts.

This is not merely a pedagogical counsel which I permit myself to express; it follows from the nature of understanding itself. For the "way," the "method," of understanding emerges from the nature of the *subject* which I am to understand. The ways of understanding a textbook of mathematics are different from those we use to understand a historical or philosophical work, and there are again different ways that apply to "holy texts." Thus in order to discover the proper hermeneutical methods I must first go through a pretheoretical, what might be called a naïve, stage of encounter with the text. I must therefore be already immersed "in the material" and have come to grips with it before I can proceed to the problems of method. This is the reason why I must not allow preoccupation with hermeneutics to *precede* concern with the text material but rather must let it *follow* it.

But as we said, hermeneutics is so fascinating and a student can so delight in his precosity that he goes on putting it in first place—and then, frequently enough, get stuck there, never pushing on to the laborious task of boring into the hard wood of the text and gaining material knowledge. We often discover this in our examinations. There it not infrequently happens that a student is able to explain to his examiners very precisely and fluently how the New Testament is to be understood—if one were to read it! But often this has not been done. These people keep fumbling with the key and know every cleft and notch in its ward, but they have never put it into the keyhole or opened or entered a door with it. Thus the result is often a rather macabre gobbledygook. These people remind me of East and West envoys discussing ticklish questions at a conference. They talk and talk about questions of method, about the agenda, about what is and what is not a legitimate subject of negotiation—and never get to the subject at all.

In order properly to assess the rank of the hermeneutical question (and this is the *only* question we are discussing here) we must also remember a *historical* fact, namely, that hermeneutics is definitely a "late" science. It corresponds exactly with that discipline in philosophy which is called "epistemology." We need only to think of the greatest epistemologist, Immanuel Kant, to realize that this is in fact a late stage in the history of thought. Man had become skeptical and lost the naïveté of simple cognition. He no longer dares to let go and simply "know" something; he sees too many examples of what comes of that—possibly a fantastic metaphysics and individual systems which are completely contradictory even though within themselves they may be completely logical and therefore *should* not contradict each other at all.

Thus there arises the question of the presuppositions of knowing, the categories that underlie it, and its radius of action. So before the reason is employed as an instrument of cognition one first investigates the instrument itself. The thinker therefore con-

cerns himself with himself and raises the question of the structure
of his organs of cognition and just what their cognitive efficiency
is. Thus he pegs out, as it were, the horizon of experience and
forbids himself to go beyond this horizon metaphysically, because
his organs of cognition are not capable of dealing with anything
beyond this region. You cannot fly to the moon in an ordinary
airplane. It was not made for this.

This is exactly what happens in the process of hermeneutics.
The person who is to understand begins to think about himself
and determines what his "organs of understanding" are capable of
and how they function. From this structure of the process of
understanding he tries to determine what can be appropriated
and what must be left out as fundamentally alien.

This tendency to introversion which is inherent in the hermeneutical question springs from the same skepticism as that of the
epistemological question: one thinks of how often one has been
mistaken in acts of understanding, how one has taken for pure
gold, taken something "as of ultimate concern for me," what was
in the end only the passing appearance of a truth or simply something hard to understand. So one begins to examine oneself.
Hermeneutics is unthinkable without skepticism and loss of
naïveté.

Naturally, this is not an objection to it. Would we say that
skeptics are worse than other people? Are they any less called to
faith? The fact is that we are actually skeptical persons precisely
to the degree that we have become mature. But then this means
that the hermeneutical question has in fact been cast in our laps
and we dare not be reactionary and act as if nothing had happened.
We cannot simply start from Reformation biblical exposition
without becoming liars. We must cross the field of hermeneutical
self-criticism and we cannot get around it. We must find our
way through to a second naïveté precisely by carrying our reflection to its ultimate conclusion.[15]

[15] Heinrich von Kleist said some very profound things about this is his
Marionettentheater.

My reference to hermeneutics and epistemology as latecomers in the history of thought was not meant as a disparagement. My intent was only to make it clear that we must not idealize them, that philosophy itself is *more* than epistemology, and that theology itself is *more* than hermeneutics. Both epistemology and hermeneutics are a kind of unpleasant necessity. We must accept them and come to terms with them. But we dare not make a virtue of this necessity and act as if now for the first time the hidden theme of all theology has become clear.

CLOSING COMMENT OF THE MODERATOR: Many thanks. My own pedagogical misgivings have now become even more pronounced, though my view was similar to yours. Our young people certainly have not gone as far in this direction as in your country, or only in exceptional cases. I have the impression, however, that the development is moving in this direction among us too. Therefore it is good for us to receive a certain warning. We do not want to evade the hermeneutical question but rather to relativize it. May we put it that way? We want to give it a proper but limited importance. I thank you.

IV

The Virgin Birth

ON THE BINDINGNESS OF DOGMAS. THE SIGNIFICANCE
OF MIRACLES. TRUE AND FALSE FAITH

QUESTION: One of the professors at our student conference stated that the doctrine of the Virgin Birth—the Christmas miracle—is one of the central dogmas of the Christian faith. He defended the thesis that our attitude toward this doctrine determines whether we believe in Christ as the Lord and the Son of God or whether Christ is regarded merely as a pinnacle of humanity as in liberal theology. What is your position with respect to this problem?

Connected with this is a second question which I would like to add. A number of the participants in the discussion put forward biblical and theological arguments against this thesis that the Virgin Birth deserves such a key position in our faith. But in the debate that broke out on this question there was *one* argument that troubled me, quite apart from this particular question. In the Apostles' Creed, it was argued, the phrase "born of the Virgin Mary" has at least equal rank with the other articles of faith, such as "I believe in Jesus Christ his only Son our Lord," who "suffered under Pontius Pilate," "rose again from the dead," "ascended into heaven," and so on. Now the argument that emerged in the debate and which seriously troubles me is this: If you take *one* stone out of this edifice of dogmas, the whole thing will begin to break down, especially if it is a cornerstone. Then you can never hold on to anything and you can no longer assert with certainty that the rest must be kept, though only this one thing must be given up.

This leads me, then, to my second question, which is naturally connected with the first: Do not all the dogmas have to be treated alike and then also be regarded as equally binding? Or are there various rankings? And if so, can one perhaps dispense with a second-class dogma?

I am afraid that this involves still a third question: If there is such a thing as this kind of graduated scale, by what right and by what criteria is this classification made?

I beg your pardon for asking so many and such demanding questions. Yet they seem to me to belong together. Not a few of us are disturbed by them. Besides, I believe that these questions constitute something like a test case in the discussion between the fundamentalist-minded Christians and those who are more liberal-minded. I therefore do not ask it merely out of personal curiosity.

ANSWER: I am not at all disturbed by the length of your question even though I am now obliged to deliver almost an entire lecture in order to give even a relatively adequate answer to it. The very basic character of the question shows that the questioner has set his problem in a larger context, apart from which it actually cannot be dealt with at all. And just because this context is taken into account, it is evident that this is not a case of "cheap doubt" but rather a matter of faith responsibly inquiring into its foundations. Woe to him who does *not* dare to doubt in this sense. Paradoxical as that may sound, it is really true that he who does not dare to doubt is not—contrary to appearances—being *true* to his faith, but is actually repressing his doubt because of *unbelief*. That is to say, he is afraid that there may be a truth which disproves his faith because it is stronger than his faith. He therefore keeps this possibility at arm's length and thus represses the doubt. But is not this repression a vote of nonconfidence in him in whom he says he believes and who called himself the truth and the life? He who represses his doubt is actually not trusting his faith; he is anything but faithful. And I would think he had every reason to distrust it.

For quite obviously, a faith which must be preserved by screening it off in this way is not a trusting affirmation of the King of truth, but merely an inner attitude, a psychic process which is supposed to run smoothly and therefore must be guarded against any disturbance. If Christ *himself* is really the object of my faith, then I need not have any fears about him, then I can doubt and question without reservations, then for me there are no longer any problems that are taboo. For then I believe in him who answers for my faith and guarantees it. Then I do not have to worry about it any more, then my retreat is secure. For then my faith no longer depends upon my psyche, which is supposed to produce this undisturbed faith, but rather upon him who wills to be faithful to me and who called blessed the poor in spirit.

So when I face him I can really say: I believe, dear Lord, help my unbelief. I can say this because I am convinced that he can really help my unbelief and that as the King of truth he can make his truth to prevail in me. Therefore I cannot have faith in my own faith; this would lead only to a kind of dogged but anxious holding on; it would turn my faith—as Luther expressed it—into a legalistic work, a seemingly God-pleasing act of man, and this would be the very thing that deprived it of its real nature. For faith is not a good work, but is the exact *alternative* of good works.

No, I cannot have faith in my own faith; I can only cast myself —perhaps in despair—upon him in whom I believe, and I must trust that he will not let me be put to shame.

I think that this can be better expressed in Greek than is possible in English or in German. For in Greek the words "faith in God" and the "faithfulness of God" sound exactly alike. It may be pointed out to those who enjoy Greek grammar that in one case the term God occurs in the objective genitive and in the other in the subjective genitive. But I find it such a wonderful thing that this linguistic identity of two terms is thus possible, that, in other words, my faith is only the subjective correlate of the attitude which God takes toward me. Therefore I must treat him in the same way. I must really let my faith be concentrated upon God. My faith must really look *away* from itself; for what I am dealing with is the faithfulness of God and thus with something that is unswerving and continuing.

Therefore I do not need to watch anxiously over my faith. I do not have to keep observing it to see whether it is now stronger and then weaker, whether it feels secure and then again is oppressed by doubts. Even when I do not think of it—perhaps because I am filled to the brim of my soul with urgent and pressing things—God is still thinking of me, encompassing me with his continuing faithfulness. I recall the words of the English soldier who in the very tumult of battle prayed, "O Lord, if I forget thee, do not thou forget me."

So a sure sign that I trust the faithfulness of God and that I know that it is there behind me is the fact that I can dare to doubt and to know that, no matter what abysses open up before me, no matter how deeply I threaten to fall, God is deeper than every abyss and down in every depth he is there to uphold me.

Here we meet with what I would call the dialectic of faith: the truth can never be stronger than my faith. Therefore I dare to doubt without having to be afraid that the King of faith will slip away from me. My courage to doubt is therefore precisely the courage of my *faith* (and not the opposite of faith!), because I know that he in whom I believe will triumph no matter what happens. Though exposed in flank and rear, I can doubt without any safeguard, because he "besets me behind and before" (Ps. 139:5).

I am afraid that the length of my answer is more than properly proportioned to the length of the question that was asked. In any case you see that I feel compelled to put our problem into an even broader context. It is, after all, a problem of doubt. I think I perceived a note of hidden anxiety behind the question. Hence so much depends upon our taking the time to reflect upon the theological and spiritual place of doubt. I may content myself with the following statement:

Faith is not identical with the attempt to consider as many things as possible to be true and to give up nothing that appears to belong to the traditional stock of faith. Such an attempt could well be a forced human work and thus not be faith at all. Therefore it is altogether logical that this attempt be connected with a particular fear, namely, the fear that the whole structure of faith may collapse if one stone is removed. If I believe in him who is the Lord of this structure, this fear is absurd—just as absurd as the disciples' fear that the ship could go down when the Lord was sleeping in it.

On the other hand, if I view the structure as an architectural edifice which is founded upon *man's* consciousness of faith and act of faith, then I surely will have to stop every day to count the stones, test its balance, put in more steel girders, and keep shoring it up so that no shock or tremor may seriously endanger this citadel of my security. But then it would certainly cease to be the "mighty fortress" of God, which I trust because I trust *him*. It would rather have become a figment of human creation, the instability of which I would rightly distrust.

This subtle change in our attitude of faith is not easy to see from the outside. The psychic forms of real faith and false faith look devilishly alike. And from the outside the false faith, which is bent only upon conservation, even looks stronger and more uncompromising than true faith, like everything that is static, which at first sight always appears to be strong enough to outlast the ages. And yet, under the surface appearance of two things that look alike, faith has been transformed from a movable and moving thing which casts itself upon the heart of the Lord into a concrete buttress poured by man in his unbelieving fear and all too human need for security—rigid, cold, and far from convincing.

Therefore, we have every reason, for the *sake* of faith (and by no means against it!), to raise the question whether the Virgin Birth is a binding doctrine.

In the light of the approach to the question which we have worked out, the decision can be made only at one point, namely, the question whether this "dogma" has constitutive importance for my believing that Christ is for me the King of the truth or not. If without this dogma I could no longer "call Christ my Lord," this would prove that it is constitutive in character. But if this confession of him as my Lord, as the one who died and rose again for me, remains untouched by the continuance or noncontinuance of this dogma, then this would show that it is of secondary importance and *not* constitutive for my faith.

In those two sentences, in which I have tried to define the method of approaching the question, I have already taken a position with regard to a problem which was inherent in the question that was posed, namely, whether there are various ranks of dogmas or whether they all have the same degree of importance. In my first answer to the question of method I indicated that I am indeed convinced of the necessity of distinguishing dogmatic *degrees* and therefore of differentiating between fundamental and more secondary doctrines. If you study a Catholic system of dogmatics, you will observe that every dogma is actually provided with a dogmatic mark or "note" and that thus there is a whole hierarchy of gradations.[1]

The differences in degree of validity are arrived at here by means of a criterion which is different from that which I have

---

[1] Some readers may be interested in these "notes" indicating the relative importance of doctrines in Catholic theology; I therefore mention them here.

Note 1: Propositio de fide (dogma). This refers to dogmas which are based upon an indubitably revealed truth, whether they have been expressly defined as such by the church or whether the "infallible" teaching of the church has expressly established them as Catholic truth.

Note 2: Propositio fidei proxima (a truth which is very near to being an article of faith). The substance of the truth contained in such an article must in the almost unanimous judgment of the theologians be contained in the sources of revelation, so that it demonstrates itself through a more or less obvious explanation. The almost negligible difference of degree between this and *Note 1* arises only from the fact that the church itself has not yet expressly defined it as revealed truth.

Note 3: Propositio theologice certa ad fidem pertinens (an article which with theological certainty pertains to faith). Such a statement counts as being closely connected with dogma (though the manner of its connection is left open), and to that extent its character as truth is assured.

Note 4: Sententia communis (common opinion). These refer to theses which are generally accepted by the theologians.

The same degrees appear again in their negative form in the evaluation of heretical statements which are to be flatly or more mildly condemned.

just proposed, that is to say, not from the point of view of whether they are constitutive for statements about the King of the truth, about the person and work of Christ. On the contrary, they are determined by the completely formalistic criterion of how close these doctrines come to the "infallible teaching of the church" or how far they depart from it.

But much more worthy of our attention is a completely different way of distinguishing degrees of validity. I am referring to the way in which Wilhelm Herrmann—who, incidentally, was the teacher of Bultmann and Barth—distinguished between the basis, or foundation, of faith (*Glaubensgrund*) and the thoughts about, or arising from, faith (*Glaubensgedanken*). Thus he differentiated between theological articles which are *fundamental* for our faith (by which this faith *lives*) and others in which one thinks theological *thoughts* about these fundamental truths (in which one therefore comments upon them, supplements, illustrates, and explains them). Then, naturally, the second kind of theological statement is much less binding. Illustrations and comments can, of course, be influenced by the times in which they are put forth, even if they are in the Bible. Thus it can happen that in a different time with the aid of a different stock of conceptions it will be interpreted differently.

I mention only one example which will illustrate what I mean. In Galatians 4:21 ff. Paul is trying to make clear the distinction between law and gospel and to show its basis in sacred history. To this end he speaks of two sons of Abraham, one by his wife who was a free woman, and the other by his maidservant Hagar. He identifies the name "Hagar" with Mount Sinai, the place where the law was given and where the impulse to slavish obedience originated. But free woman, the wife Sarah becomes for Paul an allegory of the heavenly Jerusalem in which the freedom of the Gospel dwells. According to Paul, then, we Christians belong in this second line of descent. We are the children of Isaac, the son of the free woman, whereas the slaves of the law are the children of Hagar, who dwell under the influence of Mount Sinai.

Now we shall certainly not be doing any wrong to the venerable Apostle when we say that here he has used "thoughts about faith," which were conditioned by his time, in order to describe the "foundation" of our faith, namely, the distinction between law and gospel which is fundamental and essential for our faith. That is to say, the historically trained theologians recognize immediately that Paul is here employing a very definite rabbinical method of interpretation and that he is here giving to the two descendants of Abraham an allegorical meaning which is no longer immediately apparent to us today. We could perhaps put it this way: We accept the actual *theme* of what Paul is saying, that is, we accept from him the distinction of law and gospel which is truly a "foundation of faith." We therefore reiterate what he intends to say, what he proclaims to us as a basis of faith. But we hesitate to pursue with the same firmness the "thoughts of faith" with the *aid* of which he illustrates this "foundation."[2]

Thus it would appear to me that here Wilhelm Herrmann makes a very suggestive distinction between degrees of bindingness and that it is at least possible to *discuss* a differentiation between the foundation of faith and thoughts arising from faith. But, of course, this is where the real problem begins. For now the question is where the boundary between the two lies. And at this point our agreement with Wilhelm Herrmann immediately ceases. Thus it ceases at the first occasion where his distinction should prove itself concretely. For it is certainly a complete reversal of the New Testament message when he says, for example, that the resurrection of Christ is not to be counted as one of the "foundations of faith" but is rather only a "thought arising from faith," that is to say, a thought and a conception by the aid of which the disciples made it clear to themselves that there was something more and something other in this unique life than in a normal human existence and that his death, too, meant something more and other

[2] Another example of this method is our position with regard to Paul's regulations concerning dress in church. I have discussed this in *The Ethics of Sex* (New York: Harper & Row, 1964), p. 281.

than ordinary human death or even the death of a martyr.

Here already we have a preannouncement of what is later said in Bultmann far more directly, namely, that the Easter message is only a commentary on Golgotha—and thus a more or less figurative reflection engaged in by someone who already believes or who finds his way through to his potential faith with the help of this reflection, but for whom this reflection can by no means be a "foundation" of faith.

Therefore, much as I would like at this point to advocate a differentiation between fundamental and less important articles of faith and however helpful Herrmann's distinction between "foundation of faith" and "thoughts of faith" appears to me to be—extreme caution is required here. This distinction can very quickly change from a theological truth into a temptation. It is, of course, nothing more than an empty form and the real decisions are made when we face the question of what we put into this form. What Herrmann does with it will certainly not do.[3]

Thus I have gradually worked my way to the real theme of our question: the Virgin Birth. You will certainly have the impression that here a rather fussy German professor is at work, exhausting you with endless preliminary comments and demanding such a strenuous march to the battlefield that when you finally get there you have no strength left. I suggest therefore that we have a brief intermission and go out for a while to enjoy the California sun. When you hear Bruce Gaston playing the piano—the loudspeaker will carry it outside—you are asked to come back for more.

CONTINUATION AFTER THE INTERMISSION:
I think I see a number of red faces. This may perhaps be due not

[3] On Herrmann's interpretation see my essay "The Resurrection Kerygma" in *The Easter Message Today, Three Essays* by Leonhard Goppelt, Helmut Thielicke, and Hans-Rudolf Müller-Schwefe (New York: Thomas Nelson & Sons, 1964), pp. 92 ff. [References to Herrmann's distinction can be found in his *Systematic Theology*, tr. by Nathaniel Micklem and Kenneth Saunders (New York: The Macmillan Comany, 1927), and *The Communion of the Christian with God*, tr. by J. Sandys Stanyon (New York: G. P. Putnam's Sons, 1906). Trans.]

only to the fresh air but also because the discussion outside may have grown a bit warm. But now I propose to tackle the real theme with no digressions.

After all that has been said, the real foundation of faith is my being able to say in the words of the oldest creed: Christ is Lord. But I cannot say this without at the same time making statements about Christmas and Easter (to name only two fundamentals). For he is *the* Lord and he is *my* Lord by reason of the fact that in him God himself meets me, condescends to me in love, enters into my history and endures its pressures with me, shares in my suffering and death, and thus was "found in human form."[4] Hence I can say that Jesus is Lord only because it is a miracle that he is a man like you and me. What for us is normal and therefore becomes the content of the simplest kind of ontological statement, namely, that you and I are men, is in this case a great miracle, the unheard-of exception. For here the Eternal Word comes into my flesh, here the "abnormal" occurred—that *God*—how incredible!— should become man.

> He whom the world could not inwrap
> Yonder lies in Mary's lap—

this is the way Martin Luther's Christmas hymn responds to that miracle.

We moderns have to make a real effort to get this clear in our minds; for since the earlier centuries a change has taken place in man's consciousness on this point. That is to say, it is relatively easy for us to think of Jesus as a man "like you and me," and we are moved by the fact that he suffered and died for us on the cross. That's why the churches are filled on Good Friday—at least in Germany where the memory of Jesus' death is honored on a high holiday. For us it is far more difficult to believe in his exaltation on Easter, because to many people this is all too supernatural, too superhuman, too "divine." In the earlier centuries it was quite the opposite. The assertion that Christ came from the Father in

---

[4] Phil. 2.

eternity was largely accepted as self-evident. (Actually this must be stated with far more recognition of the complexity of the situation, but it is sufficient for our purpose here.) But that he should have become completely *man*, that he came to us through a human birth and really endured suffering and death—this seemed to not a few of our Christian forefathers to be simply inconceivable. And sometimes they indulged in some extremely subtle, even cunning, experiments in terminology in order to surround him with an ultimate reservation of the divine to preserve him from entering into the "human-all-too-human." Thus there was a passionate struggle in favor of this kind of incarnation. Men were divided in these controversies and the effects were felt even in imperial politics. One need only to think of the battles over the Creed of Chaledon (A.D. 451) and the controversies between the Alexandrians and the Antiochians. But I will not trouble you with that now!

We should undoubtedly do injustice to these people who fought so passionately and with such extreme devotion over these questions if we were to see their motive as being merely a liking for subtleties and dogmatic hairsplitting. Only someone who has very superficially skimmed through the compendiums in which the bewildering formulations are simply strung together like a bizarre string of pearls without making it clear what the real issue was could make such a judgment.

What was the issue? It was nothing other than to bring out with utter clarity this one thing—that Jesus Christ is Lord. The decision whether this comes out clearly or not depended, and still depends on the question whether Jesus Christ is only a specially superior example of the human species, who was therefore called by God to special honors and services, *or* whether in him God himself meets us, whether in Jesus Christ he enters with loving condescension into our history and becomes our brother. And my understanding of the Christmas miracle depends upon whether I accept the one or the other. So what is at stake here is the whole thing, what is at issue is the "*foundation* of faith." And this explains the tremendous concern displayed in those controversies.

Again in the Easter message the whole is at stake. We have only to read the fifteenth chapter of I Corinthians to see the intellectual vehemence with which Paul expresses the alternatives which are posed by the Easter message. If the resurrection of Christ is a *fact*, even though it surely falls outside the chain of normal, objectifiable events, if here God really acknowledged his *Son* through an *act*, then our temporal and eternal destiny is affected at its depth by what happened there. But if all this is merely a legend, a dream, an interpretive thought, then "we are of all men most to be pitied," then, says Paul, we are deceived deceivers. Incidentally, then, it may well be that our generation must go through its Chalcedon on this point.

This one thing, therefore, we can be sure of and that is that the miraculous birth of Jesus Christ is constitutive of faith in his person; it is the *conditio sine qua non* for my being able to say "Christ is Lord." And this is true even when I learn to say this sentence before I understand the miracle of his birth. In the "context of being" the birth has the primacy over this sentence. In the "context of cognition" the order may be different. The Father's house not only has many mansions, it also has many entrances; but it has only one foundation.

And now the curtain rises once more in our drama of thought. (I warn you, however, that it is still not time to turn the lights on!) For now the question arises: Is everything that is reported to us about this birth—let us say, the entire scenery of Bethlehem and the events of Christmas night, which are so familiar to us from the second chapter of Luke—is all of this, without distinction, likewise marked with the brand "foundation of faith"? Or must we again make distinctions within this context? With regard to the central point of the question that was asked we can now (but note that we could not really do this until now) formulate the question as follows: If the miraculous birth of the Lord belongs among the foundations of faith which are constitutive of his Lordship, is then the Virgin Birth on its part also a foundation of faith, an indispensable condition of my being able to believe in the miraculous birth? This, I think, defines the problem very precisely.

What is undoubtedly to be characterized as a "foundation of faith," upon which all the statements concerning the unique and miraculous existence of Jesus Christ depend, is certainly the phrase in the Creed which says he was "conceived by the Holy Ghost." For that phrase means that the Lord proceeded from God, that he was not simply one who was called—who received his call, say, at his baptism—but rather that he was stamped from the beginning by a unique mode of being, namely, by the fact that in him the Eternal Word became flesh and came into our history. This statement about the nature of the Christ-event is, as we saw, not possible at all without a statement about its beginning—a statement which is in fact expressed with all the clarity that could be desired in the phrase "conceived by the Holy Ghost."

And now we sharpen our question still further: Is the sequel "born of the Virgin Mary" a necessary correlate which is inseparably bound up with the preceding phrase "conceived by the Holy Ghost"? Is it, so to speak, the biological complement without which the other phrase would hang in the air and thus lose its basis, its "foundation"?

Certainly it would be altogether misleading to think of the Virgin Birth as a kind of biological prerequisite for conception by the Holy Spirit. To wish to set up a "precondition" for a miracle, even though this precondition consists in another miracle, a preparatory miracle, would be to contradict the nature of everything the New Testament tells us about the interventions of God in the course of the world.

Rather we must give this statement of the Virgin Birth a completely different theological locus. Instead of being an explanatory precondition, it should have the significance of a "sign," which accentuates the miraculous entrance of Jesus into our life and our human history. By interpreting it as a "sign" we give to it the *nature* of all miracle. For, after all, the nature of it is to communicate a message and thus to exercise the same function as the spoken word itself. This is why the miracles of the New Testament share the same fate as the spoken word and are by no means greater than the spoken word. It is true, however, that one can be tempted for a moment to suppose that they should be more and greater than "mere" spoken words. Are they not a demonstration which can be "seen," whereas the spoken word can only be "believed"? We must consider this for a moment before we proceed.

When Jesus forgave the sins of the paralytic,[5] there arose among the clerics who were present a disparaging muttering, the purport of which was: "This claim to be able to forgive sins is blasphemy. Only God, never a man, can do such a thing." And Jesus immediately met this objection by asking: "Which is easier, to say to the paralytic, 'Your sins are forgiven,' or to say 'Rise, take up your pallet and walk'?" The expected answer to this question is obvious: naturally healing is "harder" than merely forgiving sins, for the very simple reason that the forgiveness of sins is, so to speak, an "inner" process, the actual occurrence of which cannot be checked. The healing of a cripple, however, if it really takes place, is something that can be "outwardly" seen and verified by the doctors. It would appear (though it really only *appears* to be so) to follow from this that a miracle is meant to be something superior to mere spoken words.

One might perhaps characterize this something more which is seemingly inherent in a miracle in this way: I have to "believe" the word, in this case the word of forgiveness, but I can "see" a miracle. And naturally, seeing would surpass believing. After all, seeing is part of the eschatological fulfillment which one day will supersede faith.[6] And yet it is *not* correct that we should think that miracles ought to surpass faith by providing sight and, so to speak, anticipating the eschaton. That this is actually *not* so will become clear if we examine for a moment what I said about miracle "sharing" the fate of the spoken word. That is to say, miracle confronts us with the decision between belief and unbelief exactly as does

[5] Mark 2:5.
[6] I Cor. 13; II Cor. 5:7.

the spoken word. In no way does it supplant this alternative, whereas seeing actually does supplant it; for in the eschaton, where seeing will really take place, this alternative will no longer be there. There faith will be *permitted* to see what it believed, and unbelief will be *compelled* to see what it did not believe. But when a miracle occurs, people are by no means automatically convinced by what they perceive with their senses, by what they can, so to speak (but actually only so to speak), "see." For the miracle, too, delivers them up to the alternative of believing or disbelieving.

This is evident in the fact that when the people were confronted with a miracle, they often remained doubters, exactly as they had when they heard the spoken word, indeed, their doubt may actually have been intensified. They perhaps did not doubt what they saw, but they did doubt whether it was *God* who had spoken. They considered it possible that it might rather be demonic and occult forces which were at work here. They asked the doubting question: "By what authority are you doing these things?" meaning: Is God or the devil back of them?[7] Thus their doubt is actually intensified.

The spoken word was capable of confronting them with the alternative "truth or fraud." In the face of the miracle, however, they were confronted with the real theme of faith, namely, the far more radical alternative "God or the devil."

Miracle is therefore *not* more than the spoken word, but shares its fate. It too is only the vehicle of a message which confronts men with decision and by no means makes this decision unnecessary. It merely demonstrates the message of the spoken word. In this incident of Jesus and the paralytic, for example, it points out that Jesus' words "Your sins are forgiven" are not merely teaching about the nature of the forgiveness of sins but the actual bestowal of forgiveness. The miracle is an illustration of, and commentary on, the fact that the spoken word actually performs what it says. Therefore it is itself a form of the spoken word. It contains a message.

[7] Matt. 21:23 ff.; 9:34; 12:24.

You understand, then, what I meant when I said that it is impossible that the meaning of the Virgin Birth should consist in a kind of biological prerequisite for Jesus' conception by the Holy Spirit. I said that its meaning lies rather in its character as a sign. It has the message-character of miracle. It is a word of attestation. And it proclaims that here God is at work.[8]

But even this does not cover everything that needs to be clarified here. For now the real question arises: Who set up this sign— God himself or man? (Here "man" means the primitive church, to which the tradition of this statement possible goes back, and which may have wished to bear witness to the Lord's conception by the Holy Spirit in the form of a sign.)

And here, to be completely frank about it, I do not know. Here my fellow theological thinkers leave me in the lurch. Their opinions are almost too completely at odds. And the line between the various opinions is by no means identical with the line where the conservative theologians who believe in the Scriptures and revelation separate from the more liberal, "modern" theologians who favor the existential interpretation. I refrain here from giving you samples of this variance of opinion, and, as I said, I confess that here I am in a state of indecision.

Indecision is generally not an attitude which commands much respect and you may be surprised at how decidedly and with what little shame I confess to my indecision.

The reason for my "decided indecision" is that I believe I can justify this indecision as an objectively proper attitude.

The main reason why I believe that I do not need to blush because of this indecision is, of course, that I am convinced that the Virgin Birth—unlike the affirmation of Christ's conception by the

---

[8] The Nicene Creed says something more, in a figurative way, concerning the "how" of God's being at work here, and again not with the intent of explaining something, but rather to bear witness to a particular aspect of Christology. It says concerning Christ's entrance into the world that he was "begotten" of the Father, "not made" (*genitus, non factus*). This statement means that Christ is raised above the context of creaturehood, including *human* creaturehood, and is in a privileged way the "Son" of God.

Spirit—is not a "foundation of faith" but rather a possible "thought arising from faith," and that I therefore leave undecided the question whether here God himself spoke, acted, and as it were commented on his action, or whether men were here responding to him in faith and setting forth in a metaphor what they believed. And in order to substantiate this, I do not need to point only to what I have already said, above all with regard to the ontological primacy of the witness to the conception by the Spirit; I have several other reasons in reserve.

In the first place, I may point out that only Matthew[9] and Luke[10] present the testimony of the Virgin Birth and that this testimony (though it is not unknown, nevertheless) plays no part in the rest of the New Testament, and that in John and Paul the entrance of Christ into our humanity is presented in quite a different way. Besides the positive interest in wanting to bear witness to something definite through the Virgin Birth, the recourse to a tradition of prophecy, namely, to the expectation that the coming Saviour would be the son of a virgin,[11] is also quite obviously a controlling factor. This very conclusion then also imparts to the Virgin a fundamental theological meaning, if we take it that it was believing *men* who were here giving testimony in the form of a sign. But, as we said, this can be stated in this way only if one is convinced that the Virgin Birth is not an independent fact of salvation, on the facticity of which our faith depends. It can be so stated only if one can also understand it as a possible metaphor in which faith, which is grounded upon other facts (and *really* upon other *facts*), "expresses" itself.

The question whether it was *God* who here erected a sign to awaken faith or whether it was believing *man* who erected a sign for the Son of God is one that can remain undecided for still another reason. If one takes the Virgin Birth to be a real event, then its sign-character consists in this fact, among others, that its pur-

[9] Matt. 1:18.
[10] Luke 1:35.
[11] Cf. Isa. 7:14, Septuagint.

pose is to testify to the miracle of conception by the Spirit by
pointing to the *way* in which the event happened. Then we should
have to say that it is characteristic of this way of describing how
the event occurred that it excludes the co-operation of man and
that God performs the miracle of Christ's birth, not *within* the
context of natural generation, but rather in the form of a supernatural *break-through* and thus in the form of a supernatural intervention.

If I may venture to use a rather bold figure of speech and speak
of the "style" of God's action, I must say that at this point I have
some real inhibitions with regard to the "real" character of the
Virgin Birth (as a sign erected by *God*). For this kind of reflection upon the "how" of the event is completely inappropriate to
the usual "style" of miraculous events in the New Testament. We
have only to think of the Nicodemus story. Here in this dialogue
with Jesus the question of the "miracle of rebirth" arises. And
already Nicodemus is reflecting upon the "how": "How can a
man be born when he is old? Can he enter a second time into his
mother's womb and be born?"[12] Can he begin once more from
the beginning, can he get beyond his own nature? And to this
question of "how" and "whether" Jesus answers by further "describing" (not "explaining"!) the mystery and speaking of the new
birth through the Spirit. Nevertheless Nicodemus again poses his
question of "how," and this time very bluntly, "How can this be"[13]
But again he received no answer, but had to be content with the
testimony *that* God so loved the world. . . .[14] *That* someone can
be reborn of the Spirit and *that* he, like Christ, can be born of
the Spirit—this remains a mystery of God's action which is not
and cannot be inquired into. We cannot go back and inquire behind this.

We also find this same reticence with regard to the "how" in

[12] John 3:4.
[13] John 3:9.
[14] John 3:16.

Jesus' own words about his origin: "When he spoke of his Father, he did not explain the way in which his life had its origin in God; but his oneness with God was not therefore a dark mystery to him, not something he merely thought, wished, and hoped; but rather he knew with a shining certainty that his life had its ground in God. The miracle that created him was manifest to him in the fact of his life. He who removes it from the history of Jesus simply takes away from the Christmas story the foundation on which it stands. But what he then envisages is something different from that which happened." These are not my words but those of Adolf Schlatter on this subject.[15]

And, finally, it makes some impression upon me to see that Luther too leaves this question to some extent open. He said of the Virgin Birth: "It does not make much difference whether she was a virgin or a wife, though God willed that she be a virgin."[16] He therefore quite obviously does not think of the Virgin Birth as a constitutive fact of salvation. From this point of view it is an adiaphoron. True, he accepts it, but not for "theological" reasons, but, so to speak, positivistically, on the basis of the pure fact that is so written. But the theological question of the *rank* of the statement is clearly in the background.

QUESTION: If it is true that the article of the Virgin Birth does not have the same rank as the article "conceived by the Holy Ghost," ought we not be honest about it and strike it out of the Creed? I would think that such a creed should contain only statements of faith which are completely unequivocal and indubitable. ANSWER: Not long ago someone said to me that on Sunday when the congregation recites the Apostles' Creed he simply could not say the words "born of the Virgin Mary," that he simply could not understand or accept this statement. When I asked him what the nature of his difficulties with it were, he replied that he did

[15] *Hülfe in Bibelnot*, p. 109.
[16] *WA* 15, 411, 21-23.

not know what exactly they were himself; that perhaps they were
of a rationalistic kind (though it would be rather arbitrary to
attach his doubts only to *this* particular statement); that perhaps
his difficulty also lay in the fact that he simply did not know what
to do with this article and that as far as the Christmas message was
concerned it appealed only to his emotions. But for this very
reason he had become distrustful of himself and felt that he ought
to be honest about it.

After all that I have said here, you can perhaps guess what my
answer to him was. I rather astounded him by confessing that it
was not clear to me whether this sign was erected by God or by
men, whether therefore it was an act of God which demanded our
faith or whether it was a figurative expression brought forth by
man's faith. I explained to him why I did not consider this distinction conclusive (at this *one* point, let it be understood, and by
no means generally). But whatever may be the case with this
alternative, the statement concerning the Virgin Birth is not meant
to be a biological explanation, a statement about the "how" of the
event, but rather a communication of a *sign*—a sign that Jesus
Christ is not a man who was called like a prophet to the service
of God, but rather that in him God himself entered among us,
that he gave us his only begotten Son, and that here there occurred
the miracle of a love that comes into our strange land and takes its
place beside us. It is this miracle that I acknowledge and it is to
this Son of God that I pray when I give my reverence to the sign
of the Virgin Birth and bear witness to it in my saying of the
Creed. When I do this I join with the shepherds and the wise men
from the East in adoring the miracle of Bethlehem. And if I am
unsure about the "whether" and the "how" of the sign, I nevertheless look to him to whom the sign points, to "The eternal
Father's only Son," as Luther's Christmas hymn says.[17] I look to
the "new sunshine' that comes from the "eternal light," and I
worship him " whom the world could not inwrap" and now "lies
in Mary's lap." So why should I not say with joy the words "born

[17] *"Gelobet sei'st du, Jesus Christ"* (Praise be to thee, Jesus Christ).

of the Virgin Mary," and why should there be any point at all where I could not join the chorus of the Christmas hymns?

QUESTION: I hope it is not too presumptuous, considering the very comprehensive answer we have been given and the lateness of the hour, if I ask another question which was prompted by your reply. Did I understand you rightly as saying that in your presentations you wished to maintain the following propositions: The obedience of faith does not consist in simply accepting the dogmas of the church on the basis of its higher authority, but that our faith must rather be critical and dare to doubt?

ANSWER: You did understand me aright. You are doubtless familiar with the way in which Luther passionately resisted the notion that faith means "holding something to be true" (and possibly even a summary kind of assent in the sense of giving blanket authority to the church). When he said this, however, there were two things he did *not* want to say. He was not giving the green light to a rationalistically motivated doubt, and he was not denying that our faith is based upon histroical facts in which God really acted. There could be no worse misunderstanding of Luther's polemic against the notion that faith is merely assenting to or holding something to be true than to read out of it the thesis (set forth, for example, by Lessing) that we do not need to adhere to historical facts or what is perhaps the mere *assertion* of seemingly historical and largely supernatural facts, but rather that we may allow ourselves to be persuaded only by "universal truths of reason," for these truths are "convincing" in themselves; they do not need to be "regarded" as true, they do not require a sacrifice of the intellect; but rather they are simply evident and they call forth a spontaneous intellectual agreement.

These truths of reason are precisely the thing which the revelation of God is not concerned with. It is rather concerned with communications about the mightly acts of God, which someone has to tell us about, which we cannot tell ourselves, and which we cannot construct ourselves by means of any postulate of reason whatsoever. When Luther spoke against the idea of simply "holding something to be true" he was saying something totally different from this. What he was saying is this: When a person forces himself to "hold something to be true" he is no longer dealing with faith at all. Then he is subjecting himself to the pressure of a slavish obedience (*oboedientia servilis*) and allowing himself to be cramped and constricted by intellectual repressions, whereas the very purpose of faith is to make one free.

But how does faith make us free? It does so by causing us to *trust* the one who is speaking to us and acting upon us here. But trust can never be forced; it is always a spontaneous thing. Trust cannot be *commanded* any more than love can be commanded. Both trust and love are kindled, awakened, released—and then I feel "driven" to trust and to love. Trust is something that is won from me.

But this also determines my attitude toward the historical accounts, toward the "mighty acts" of God. It would be downright perverse to think that my first act must be to force myself to regard certain accounts and dogmas as true in order finally to win my way through to the spontaneity of trust. Where has trust ever arisen in such an artificial, forced way? No, the trust of faith comes into being when these acts of God (and the accounts of them) become translucent, so that I receive them as signals of a heart that beats for me. So what must happen is what to Jesus' sorrow did not happen at the miraculous feeding of the thousands: the bread must become a sign and men must see behind the one who cares for them and is himself the bread of life.

So trust "emerges"; we must not try to "produce" it. If we must first pass through a forced act of obedience, this is proof that there really is no trust at all, but only repressed distrust.

But when the trust of faith is thus reposed in the person (the heart) of the Lord who meets me in his acts, then it may be that the beginnings will be very small indeed and that it will take a long time before one grows into the fullness of faith. But when for the first time I say Yes to him in faltering trust, when for the first time I am moved to a timid trust that he loves me and cares for me, then the decisive step has already been taken. Then I will seek to discover the Saviour in everything that is recorded about him or in what the church tells in its dogmatic teaching. Then more and more he "becomes" the truth for me and I have no need to regard something as true. Once he himself has become the truth for me, all the rest will be added to me.

Because this is so, many of the minor figures in the New Testament have often been of special comfort to me, for example, the Canaanite woman[18] and the woman with the issue of blood.[19] Neither of them holds anything to be true, for the simple reason that they hardly knew anything about which they could regard as true or untrue. They knew nothing about the rank of the figure of Jesus, they had no glimmer of a "dogmatic consciousness," and naturally not a trace of "Christology." They merely stretched out their hands to him because they trusted that he could help them and had a heart for the afflicted. The Canaanite woman even clung to her trust when he kept silent and put her trust in him to the test. And beyond this the woman with the issue of blood was steeped in superstition and made him a savior-figure in the context of her magical concept of the world. She certainly had a completely wrong notion of miracle! But all this made no difference whatsoever. It was enough that—even in the context of completely false preconceptions and a magical way of thinking—she *trusted* him. If one is close to the King of truth only in trust, there will be a process by which one can go on growing from truth to truth. The point is that one grows, that one does not do something. When a person grows, something happens to him that is completely spontaneous.

I think this is a great comfort to us and that it gives us a sense of joyful freedom. I think it releases us from the yoke of dogmatism without delivering us over to irresponsibility and noncommitment.

[18] Matt. 15:21 ff.
[19] Matt. 9:20 ff.

Not long ago a young art student said to me, "I'll tell you why I always recoil from the church. The people who go to church strike me as being so terribly cocksure. They seem to be in possession of all the mysteries of this world and the next and they literally overwhelm you with their dogmatic exuberance. I always feel so small and helpless that I'd rather not have anything to do at all with these spiritual plutocrats. It is as if I were being blinded with a thousand-watt lamp and that's simply too much and too overwhelming for a poor mole who has been burrowing through the dark earth and comes blinking into the light. A modest little candle would perhaps be the right thing. Then you could get somewhat accustomed to the light. But please, not this excruciating thousand-watt lamp."

Do you understand what the young man meant? The fact is that we can begin in a very small way. The unpretentious sign of our outstretched, empty hands is enough. Then appears the little candle that tells me that someone is reaching out for me and wants to be with me. And this hope, this trust, is the decisive beginning. Then afterward many more candles may be kindled and many other lights may go on. God is a God of growth; therefore he can begin with some very small things. And we ought not to want to be more godly than God; we should not always want, as Dietrich Bonhoeffer said, to be a step or two ahead of God. We should not be lighting whole chandeliers when he is content with a little candle. Even his Word claims to be no more than a modest lamp to our feet that lights up the next step we take today, not a big searchlight that illuminates the next couple of years. The smaller the light is that I follow at first the more will my trust be provoked—the trust that he will guide me through the dark and then lead me from light to light.

QUESTION: When you talk in this way about growing in faith, do you think it possible that even though you are a professor of theology, you may not yet have grown up fully into faith in the Virgin Birth and that some time in your life there will come a stage when you will profess it fully and without any reservations? This question is not meant in any way to be malicious or disparaging. On your level of thinking it is surely no disgrace in thinking of oneself as one who is still growing, even though one has already accomplished something in theology.

ANSWER: Certainly it is not a disgrace; and I am only grateful to you for not regarding me as a decrepit old fogy who has no further development ahead of him. But what do you mean by the words "fully and without any reservations"? I think that I am already doing this when I confess my faith in what the Virgin Birth as a sign is pointing to. Or do you regard the fact that I leave open the question whether it is a "divine or a human sign" as being a qualifying reservation?

And yet I do not want to embarrass you with this counterquestion. Perhaps it will be sufficient to say that on this point too one must be prepared for surprising changes in one's own thinking and that in any case one must keep oneself open to them. But even if I were to accept such a form of development, it would still mean only a variation within the same fundamental certainty of faith. It would neither lead beyond it nor beneath it. It would only show me another side of the one thing which it is necessary to believe. It would still be the same song, even though the key might be changed.

We see such modulations not only in our own development but also in the existence side by side of the various witnesses and theologies, such as can already be seen in the New Testament itself. There are many variations of the praise of God. The many different witnesses and the various stages of growth in faith do not make the one witness *confusing* but rather *enrich* it. At any rate they do this on the one condition that they sing these various melodies in discipleship and praise of that one miraculous act in which the Eternal Word became flesh and the Son of God became our brother.

But your question prompts me to make an altogether different observation which, particularly in this student group, concerns

me far more. Far more important, it seems to me, than the question
whether I accept or reject this (and every other) dogma is the
totally different problem of the *reason* why I say Yes or No. How
different, for example, is the Yes that a fatalist says to fate from
the Yes that I say as a Christian to the will of God! After all, the
fatalist says Yes too. He knows that there is no sense in forever
quarreling with his fate and that a man only wears himself out in
permanent opposition and constant negation. Since fate is meaningless and you can't argue with it, the best thing, he thinks, is to
give up your resistance and simply go along with it. In this sense
one can even swing oneself up (or down) to what Nietzsche called
amor fati, to "loving one's fate." This then looks like a very balanced kind of reconciliation with fate, but in reality it is only a
despairing capitulation. It is resigning oneself to something with
which there is no basis of discussion or negotiation.

One has only to express it in this way to recognize at once how
different is the Christian's acceptance of what God allows to
happen to him. He says this Yes, for example, when he says "Thy
will be done" in the Lord's Prayer. And the Canaanite woman
also spoke this "Yes, Lord," even though Jesus seemed to be silent
and to be snubbing her completely. But this is by no means a
despairing acceptance and capitulation. Here I can say Yes in
full trust, for I know *who* it is I am saying Yes to, I know that he
has a purpose in what he allows to happen to me, that his purpose
for me is good, and that I can entrust myself to him. I do not
capitulate to mindless fate and meaningless chance. I bow before
the higher thoughts of God who knows better than I myself what
I need and what will work to my good. We must therefore look
at the motive behind the Yes. When two people say the same
thing it is not always the same thing.

The same thing is true of dogmas. I can say a godless Yes to the
dogma of the Virgin Birth—and, naturally, a godless No.

I say a godless Yes, for example—and the fathers of the early
Christian centuries were often quite aware of this and were there-

fore so unyielding in their polemics—if I use the dogma of the
Virgin Birth to pander to the heresy of Docetism. Forgive me for
using this technical term, but it is not difficult to understand what
it means.

We mean by Docetism the doctrine, advocated mostly by the
ancient Gnostics, that Christ had only a phantom body, the appearance of a body,[20] that he was a heavenly being who merely
clothed himself in a human body, that he merely assumed a seeming
humanity. The Virgin Birth could then be used as a seeming confirmation of this kind of Christology, for this kind of generation
and birth seemed to shield Christ from the succession of the
generations and put him outside the realm of the human.

I should think that here it would be unnecessary for me to go
into the reasons why this is absolutely and precisely wrong at
every point in God's saving work. This is a denial of the central,
determinative issue, namely, that for love's sake Christ took upon
himself the lot of our humanity and became our brother. Here
the Word did *not* become flesh. Here I remain alone with no com-
panion in my suffering and death. Here nobody comes to seek me
out in my own highways and hedges. So all that is left for me here
is a redemption (an illusory redemption) which I must gain for
myself by purifying myself and lifting myself up through as-
ceticism and ecstasy to that supramundane being which this divine
being, Christ, never really left.

In the face of this I would dare to say that if it were a matter
of saying Yes or No to the Virgin Birth, then here a No would
be better than a Yes. For to believe in the gracious condescension
of God by saying No to it is better than to affirm it and cheat
oneself out of the central, determinative act of God. But, thank
God, we are not faced with this alternative at all; I have merely
set it up as an extreme situation.

Naturally, there is also such a thing as a godless No to the
Virgin Birth. This happens when I reject it for rationalistic reasons

[20] The word "Docetism" comes from the Greek word *dokein*, to appear.

and allow myself to be overwhelmed by the doubt that tells me that God's power has its limits and that such a biological monstrosity simply goes too far; or when, perhaps again for rationalistic reason, I stubbornly hold on to the idea that Christ can have been only a specially outstanding example of the human species and that he had his experience of being called just like other prophetic persons.

So you tell me why you say Yes or No to a truth of faith and I will tell who you are—whether you are merely a Christian conformist who says yea and amen to everything because he is too lazy to think or just existentially lazy, and then quite unjustifiedly basks in the feeling that he is a true believer and is also respected as such by the pious in the land. *Or* whether you are someone who is taking the first timid step of trust and ventures to say "Yes, Lord," who is actually afraid to believe *too much* all at once (because it might be dishonest to do so) and who nevertheless knows that the hand he has grasped will lead him from truth to truth.

We should not merely be witnesses of the faith; we should also be credible witnesses. But we shall be credible and convincing and our witness can be infectious only if we are, not merely fellow travelers, acceptors, conformist yea-sayers to the Christian tradition, but rather if we proclaim truths made our own. *To believe too much is worse than to believe too little.* For he who believes too little (and knows it and then in trust says, "Lord, I believe, help my unbelief") is subject to the promise that is given to the poor in spirit. He who puts only *one* hand in that of the Lord can confidently let his *other* hand remain empty. For he whose hand he has grasped is no meager giver; he gives abundantly. He who believes too much (or better, *thinks* he believe all this) is living beyond his spiritual means and, being a Pharisee, he comes off worse than the publican who stands afar off and knows that he can only live by grace.

I suspect that we are all amazed at the breadth of terrain we could take in and had to take in when we contemplated this one dogmatic point, the Virgin Birth. No matter through what doors or back doors we enter into the zone of the divine mysteries, we are always in the Father's house and its spacious rooms. And, touched by an unseen hand, one door after another opens up.

V

Speaking in Tongues

WHAT IS MEANT BY "FILLED WITH THE HOLY SPIRIT"?
AN ENCOUNTER WITH THE ADVOCATES OF GLOSSOLALIA

QUESTION: What do you think of speaking in tongues and baptism with the Spirit?

ANSWER: I have been told again and again on this trip about the extent to which speaking in tongues, enthusiastic ecstasy, and alleged baptism with the Spirit has "broken out" in the churches of America. And this, I have been told, has occurred not only among Negro groups (where enthusiasm has probably always played a part) but also in white congregations, and even in student groups. By my use of the term "broken out," which is identical with the verb which describes the spread of an epidemic, I have already indicated that I would relegate these phenomena to the realm of spiritual pathology. I know that Paul did not simply reject out of hand similar occurrences in the primitive church, but I also know that he did not pour any oil on these fires of the Spirit, but rather put a damper on them and cautioned restraint.[1]

The Apostle is obviously filled with a deep distrust of spiritual fruits which appear to flourish in "blessed"—or in supposedly "blessed"—union with God and cannot serve to the feeding of one's neighbor. In the last analysis the church lives in the struggle between God and Satan, between faith and unbelief. And anything which does not contribute to our strengthening in this struggle is dubious, emasculating, and useless in a deeper sense than the merely pragmatic. And it is certainly not very flattering when

[1] I Cor. 14.

in this sense Paul compares speaking in tongues with a trumpet that gives forth an unclear sound which is anything but a call to battle and rather allows the people to go on sleeping peacefully. And does not what he says about the self-edification[2] which is produced by speaking in tongues have about it an undertone of irony? Where else in the New Testament is there any reference to such self-centered culture (not to say, such cosmetics) of one's own soul? Where is there any reference whatsoever to spiritual receiving which is not meant to be immediately passed on to others? Where is there any gift which does not in the same moment become a task, a responsibility, a service to others?

Apostles too are capable of irony. And when Paul challenges his readers to interpret the speaking in tongues, that is, to translate it from ecstatic stammering into clear speech and from self-enjoyment into helpful communication, the obvious question is: Why not use clear words from the beginning, why choose this roundabout way of possibly selfish ecstasy? Manifestly the Apostle is giving us to understand that here the spiritual costs are greater than the benefits and that one is coming very dubiously close to the limit of a calculated risk.

This by no means completely concealed criticism can be understood only if the phenomenon of speaking in tongues is not isolated by itself but rather seen as a symptom of a deeper and more elemental phenomenon of spiritual life, namely "enthusiasm" (*Schwärmerei*). This again is grounded in a particular understanding of the Spirit, or more precisely, the Holy Spirit. It is true that the Holy Spirit is referred to in metaphorical terms like "wind"[3] and "fire"[4] and thus is described as something that carries a person away, a consuming and swallowing power. And yet these images must not be allowed to flourish autonomously; what must be clearly kept in view is *where* a person is being carried away and *what* is being consumed. In any case, the ecstasy as

[2] I Cor. 14:4.
[3] John 3:8.
[4] Matt. 3:11; Acts 2:3.

such is not a state which can be attributed to the power of the Holy Spirit. For taken by itself it is only an empty form which does not show *where* a person is being carried to.

Moreover, the Holy Spirit positively does *not* lead one to that state of negation of the self which the term ecstasy, which means "being beside oneself," seems to imply. If anything, one could probably say that the people of God who are gripped by the Holy Spirit really *find* themselves in a positive sense, rather than lose themselves, that they gain their real selves and, so to speak, become "originals." More precisely, they cease to be mere copies of their environment, their milieu, the spirit of their time and its idols. They find themselves in their source and in what they were created to be, in short, in their immediacy to God. Man becomes an original when he has found his *origo*, his Creator, and lives by him.

The Holy Spirit therefore leads to the finding of *oneself* through the finding of *God*. The opposite of this, that he who loses God loses himself, has always been true. The far country in which the prodigal son is lost is not only the symbol of estrangement from the father but also of estrangement from himself. In the deepest sense he also became untrue to *himself*.

The physical conception of the Holy Spirit, which can be suggested by the images of fire and wind, requires still another restriction. That is to say, these images may suggest that the Holy Spirit is a kind of attribute or quality which is imparted to me, which consequently I "patch on" to myself, which fills me, and then can become the subject of a kind of autobiography. Now it is true that the Bible uses the phrase "filled with the Holy Spirit" and the expression "indwelling of the Holy Spirit."[5] It would certainly be foolish to deny that in such moments something perceptible occurs in the psyche and that those who are thus blessed have an "enthusiastic" experience. And yet we would immediately get on the wrong track if we were to allow ourselves to be misled by this into either of two conclusions: either the idea that here the

[5] I Cor. 3:16; Luke 1:15, 41; Acts 2:4, 4:31, 13:52.

Holy Spirit becomes an "attribute of man," which one might then describe as the condition of his *holiness;* or the notion that this condition can become an object of this person's self-observation, his interest in himself, and possibly even his self-gratification.

The words "filled with the Holy Spirit" actually turn our attention *away* from the person who is filled *to* that which fills him.

But even this is not stated precisely enough. For even that which fills him with the power of God is not an end in itself. Its purpose is rather to open him up to and cause to have power over him something to which he was previously closed. All those of whom we are told that they were "filled with the Holy Spirit" suddenly discover the mighty acts of God, or better, the mighty acts of God disclose themselves to them. They receive certainty with regard to their calling, as, for example, John the Baptist. Or the whole panorama of God's sacred history opens up to them, as in the case of Peter on the day of Pentecost. Or they are given the power to confess their faith and to tell it abroad, the power of spontaneity. In every case their attention is not focused upon themselves, in order, as it were, that they may enjoy a new inner condition, but rather *outside* of themselves. The Spirit does not cause them to concentrate upon what happens *in* them but rather upon what happens to them.

Now, of course, one should not proceed to throw out the baby with the bath, as many dialecticians have done. We need not conclude that nothing at all happens *in* me and that even the terms "experience," "devout awe," and holy feeling are nothing but a Pietistic error. Such a conclusion would be quite as one-sided as the other. Naturally, there is room for this kind of cognition. How could God's history draw us into itself, how could it ever come near to us, without affecting our experience and even touching our nerves? One can push one's fear of the purely psychic so far that almost unconsciously one becomes Docetic and sober objectivity becomes, not a spiritual virtue, but a sign of stark spiritual avidity. On the other hand, we must on no account fail to see where the real focal point of the experience lies and that the experience is only a byproduct of that which happens *to* me, of what comes to me from the outside as God's action and God's history.

The way in which we respond to the experience of the Holy Spirit, of being filled with the Spirit, can actually be a criterion of our spiritual health. Does it lead me to the enjoyment of my own feelings, does it lead to introversion? If so, then I am abusing the gift of the Spirit, or I may even be confusing my own enthusiasm with the Spirit of God. Or does it cause me to leave the dark house of my previous life and leap into the "wind" which is shaking its foundations? Do I really *accept* this intervention of God in my life? Do I immediately go out to perform the service which is committed to me? Do I love and praise God and pass on to others this good Word of God?

Thus it is obviously inherent in the nature of the Holy Spirit that he does not make my psyche a kind of permanent stopping-place, but rather that he merely uses it as a station from which I must immediately depart and move on. If I am privileged to be a temple of the Holy Spirit, then this temple is the place from which I am now sent out.

Whichever statement about the Holy Spirit we examine in the New Testament, we find that all of them have this one thing in common, namely, that my attention is turned away from myself and directed to *what happens to me*, that is, the mighty acts of God.

For this turning away of attention from myself there are two other observations which are characteristic.

First, nowhere in the Bible does a person ever say about himself, "I am filled with the Holy Spirit." There is not a single sentence that begins with "I." On the contrary, this is always a conclusion drawn by *others*, whether by the hearers of the Spirit-filled proclamation or by the chronicler of a spiritual event. The person who is himself filled with the Holy Spirit has, as it were, no time to talk about it. For the Spirit who fills him has given him to see something quite different from himself. And now as he describes and proclaims this he forgets all about himself. He even forgets the state of being filled with the Spirit which caused him to see all this. Being filled with the Spirit is, so to speak, bound up with a state of self-forgetfulness.

Connected with this is the *second* observation. The way in which the Holy Spirit teaches me to become uninterested in myself and to let myself disappear behind what happens *to* me also expresses itself in some characteristic forms of speech. I can say, I "have" a Father in heaven. I can also say, I "have" a Saviour. But a strange and characteristic inhibition overtakes me when I would say I "have" the Holy Spirit. Why do I have inhibitions at this point?

It does not appear to me to be difficult to find the reason for this hesitation. When I say that I have a Father or a Saviour, it is impossible for me to do this without pointing away from myself to the one who stands over against me. Then I am no longer talking about myself, but rather glorifying someone else. I am bearing witness, like John the Baptist, to someone behind whom I must recede: "He must increase, but I must decrease."[6] But when I say that I have the Holy Spirit, the statement covertly becomes an autobiographical statement. I make the temple the subject of concern and am no longer talking about him who dwells in this temple. Then almost involuntarily the focus of attention is my good self and not the one who makes the self good.

The relationship to the Holy Spirit therefore involves its dangers; it exposes a person to temptation. As the chance grows greater so also does the risk. This is connected with the fact that the Holy Spirit has been misinterpreted as an impersonal force and that thus I can succumb to the temptation to turn the metaphors of "wind" and "fire" into independent entities. As soon as my conception of the Holy Spirit becomes that of a mere force, I forget that I am "confronted" with him and I think of myself as the "possessor" of this power. And then it is easy to understand that I will regard the possessor as being more important than what I

6 John 3:30.

possess. If I think of the Holy Spirit as something which I "have," it is inevitable that myself will immediately become important and interesting to me.

Here again certain forms of speech are very revealing. If somebody says to me, "You are a gifted man," I am inclined to blush because I take it as a flattering comment (which is very pleasing to me). But if I took this statement literally, there would not be the slightest occasion for this flattered blushing. For then I would realize that certain gifts have been *given* to me and that therefore I have had nothing to do with them at all. So instead of being flattered and saying "Thank you," I ought at once to give the thanks away and pass it on to him who has so endowed me. There is a very definite reason why as a rule I do not do this, but rather delight in this approval of myself, and that is that I regard myself as the "possessor" of gifts; I find myself interesting; and this is the only reason why I regard myself as the flattered recipient of such a comment. As soon as I think of something as a thing—whether it be an intellectual endowment or the Holy Spirit himself—I think of myself as the possessor and therefore the one who has control of it. The fact that I have received possessions and talents and that therefore he from whom I received them is far more important than I—this tends always to recede from my consciousness. And immediately we have a lovely case of egocentricity; immediately the flesh takes hold of the long side of the lever.

This misuse of the gifts of the Holy Spirit has always been the great temptation of the spiritual man. Once we realize this, the scales suddenly fall from our eyes and we begin to understand some of the dogmatic formulations which may have seemed somewhat fabricated and subtle before. We understand then, for example, why it is that in the creedal formulations of even the most ancient church it is so emphatically stressed that the Holy Spirit is the "third person" of the deity and that this was really a polemic against the misunderstanding of the Holy Spirit as a mere force (dynamics). I am always facing a person; that person challenges me to fellowship, or he severs (or *I* sever) this relationship; but I can never "possess" him.

This is why the ancient Athanasian Creed attaches such great importance to the statement that the Holy Spirit was not created but rather stands alongside of the Creator. For I might think that I could possess something created or at any rate feel that I was on the same level with it. For the same reason the first article of the Augsburg Confesson emphasizes that it is heresy to believe that the Holy Spirit is "a movement which is produced in created things" (*motus in rebus creatus*). If he were that, I could indeed "have" him; then he could be nothing more than the content of a pious experience. Luther makes exactly the same point when in his controversy with the enthusiasts he emphasizes again and again that the Holy Spirit is bound to the vehicle of the Word and that he reaches us only by means of this vehicle and not through free, unbound "blowing where he wills." But the Word (and this is the point here) always comes to me from the outside as news, as a message which I cannot tell myself and which makes me wait for him, and thus look away from myself. Hence, I cannot express my relationship to the Holy Spirit with the verb of possession "have," but only by waiting and praying: *Veni creator Spiritus*.

This, I think, is a clear formulation of the central danger: If I think of the Holy Spirit as a force (not as a person), I forget the giver, indeed, I forget the gift itself, and I become interesting to myself as one who is gifted and accordingly regard myself as important. Actually, I could be content with that statement, and yet I must at least suggest one last mystery of this demonic perversion.

We have no promise that tells us that there is anything whatsoever between heaven and earth which can surpass faith in the justifying Word. The one thing that is more than faith is sight. But seeing is an eschatological act which no longer belongs in the realm between heaven and earth, but will not occur until heaven and earth have passed away.[7] As long as we live in this aeon faith

[7] Matt. 24:35.

remains the ultimate. And this faith is characterized by the fact that it is never merely faith *in* something (namely, in that justifying Word of God which says, You are a just man to me—despite all that you actually are), but is always also faith *contrary* to something (namely, contrary to all appearances which veil God's power and righteousness, which cause him to be hidden under cover of the cross). Faith therefore always remains faith that is vulnerable, challenged, tempted. And just as we never get beyond faith, so faith never gets beyond the Psalmist's cry, "Nevertheless I am continually with thee," which it utters in the midst of temptation.

But the person who separates the Holy Spirit from the Word that awakens faith wants something more than faith alone. He wants an experience that will supplement faith or make it unnecessary. He is not content to let the Word come to him in order that it may comfort, strengthen, and make him certain of all the promises right where he is in his pilgrimage, in the midst of this strange world. Instead he wants the Spirit to lift him out of space and time, to snatch him away from himself in an ecstatic experience, to give him the gift of sight before the time comes for him to see. Thus there can be in these ecstasies a despising of the Word, a hubris which insists upon fulfillment because it is not content with the promise. Luther called this form of ecstasy, which, after all, is only a subtle form of self-dependence and is bent upon the fulfillment and enhancement of the self, the demonic worship of the *frui Deo* (the illegitimate enjoyment of God). Thus he expressed graphically and concisely what man is really out for: himself, his own pious flesh, and nothing else.

But this is the exact opposite of what is intended by "justification by faith"; for the secret of this justification is that it changes the direction in which a man looks. By nature all of us look at ourselves, our happiness and our self-fulfillment, in other words, at what we are ourselves and what happens within us. Even the so-called religious man is no exception to this. He knows, to be sure, that his deliverance and his salvation depend in one way or another upon what comes to him from God. But then he also keeps an eye on the effect which this thing that comes from God has upon him and in him. When he says that everything depends upon the grace of God (even the decrees of the Council of Trent say this!), then he watches to see how this grace shows itself in him, whether and to what extent he is the recipient of grace, whether and to what extent he is the recipient of grace, whether and to what extent the water level of grace is rising in him, whether he is performing better works, whether he has more devout feelings, whether he is making progress in his inner development. So now he becomes egocentric in a higher sense and falls again into the state of being turned in upon himself (*incurvatus in se*). This was the burden of Luther's struggles in the monastery, the thing that would give him no rest and robbed him of peace. For his critical self-observation showed him every day anew that the old Adam had by no means surrendered his sovereignty and that there was precious little or no evidence at all of a new being.

For him the real Reformation break-through did not come until Staupitz directed his attention to the Crucified and thus away from himself, thereby changing the direction of his gaze and taking away his pious egocentricity. When Luther learned that in Jesus Christ he was righteous in the sight of God and accepted by God—that this God wanted to be *his* God, even though he was unworthy—he became in a higher sense indifferent to himself and ceased being the constant subject of his self-observation. Now whatever he did in the way of good or bad works could no longer be so important, because this no longer had any effect upon the one determinative issue of his life, namely, whether he was accepted by God and whether he could stand before him. Even then his experience of faith and all his devout feelings and certainties were subject to this relativization: it was not the fact that *he* thought about God that was the ground of his salvation, but rather that *God* was thinking of him. In this sense, then, I could actually say that "justification by faith alone" consists in looking in a particular direction, no longer taking myself too seriously and concentrating on the question of what God is doing to me and for me.

We may sum it up as follows: When the Holy Spirit is known to
be God himself, where he is operative as the *Word* of God which
reveals itself to me and touches me, he never for a moment allows
me to think that he is a mere force that fills me. Then never for a
moment can I think of myself as one who is "gifted," whose own
self becomes the center of interest, and who enjoys his "gifted-
ness." Instead, he wrests my gaze away from myself and turns it
to the mighty acts of God. He causes me to see the glories of his
Word. He who wants only to hoard the riches bestowed upon him
by God's gifts of the Spirit becomes a stagnant pond with no
outlet, and the water of life turns into a swamp. God accepts only
flowing waters. I am only a channel through which the water of
God flows[8] in order to bless others. Therefore any kind of spiritual
self-enjoyment, any kind of preoccupation with self, is already an
incurvatus in se.

I said that the Holy Spirit causes us to see the glories of the
Word. Of myself I cannot see them; for the natural man sees none
of this, precisely because he is interested only in himself (in a
higher or a lower sense). Thus the work of the Holy Spirit can
be represented in the following adaptation of a familiar illustration:

Let us think of the mighty acts of God as pictures of the kind
we see in the stained-glass windows of a church. The purpose of
the artist was to allow these many-colored windows to proclaim a
message to me. If I walk around the outside of the church, the
windows look like gray panes which contain no message. Not until
I go inside and the light of day makes the colors shine do they
begin to tell a story and proclaim a message. This is the work of
the Holy Spirit: to take me inside the sanctuary where the Word
begins to shine, where it begins to speak to me and to tell me something. When I stand before these messages, I forget myself, I am
hardly conscious that it is *I* who am standing there. For I am not
in a hall of mirrors; I am confronted with messages which are far
away from my own self-concern. And even after I leave the

[8] John 7:38.

sanctuary to go to my work and to my neighbor, I am filled with tasks to perform and I have no time to think about myself. I have become free of myself (and what a liberation and what a *feeling* of liberation that is!). But then in this freedom from myself I have also found myself—in a way totally different from what I could have dreamed.

VI

The Faith of Unbelievers

WHAT ABOUT THOSE WHO CANNOT BELIEVE?

QUESTION: What happens in eternity to those who have not come
to faith in their lifetime? Does the passage "No one comes to the
Father, but by me"[1] really mean that all those for whom Christ
was not the Lord will be eternally condemned? But would not this
be the logical consequence of Christianity's claim to be absolute?
The question becomes even more distressing when we think of
those who have never heard anything about him or of those who
have heard only a caricature of his Word. When you consider that
Christ—seen from the whole sweep of history—was a relative late-
comer, the thought of it is likely to make you dizzy.

ANSWER: The dizziness that seizes a man in the face of such
questions may well be positively productive. It is, indeed, the extreme opposite pole of the kind of security and certainty that never
allows itself to be shaken and therefore will not face any questions
at all. A person who is shocked and shaken, however, is a person
who does have questions, fundamental questions. And since the
problem which has been presented is one that determines the
destiny of our faith, one that can really shake us and upset the
foundations of our life, we need to be open-minded in order really
to hear what is involved and re-examine what we have long known
or what we only seemingly knew.

If we break down the question as it was asked and define it
somewhat more precisely, we see that there are two sides to the
problem.

[1] John 14:6.

100

First, the question of what happens to the unbelieving in eternity arises from the fact that a certain number of people actually have not heard God's call to repentance and reconciliation. In order to visualize this type of person we do not have to go back to distant times before the birth of Christ; we can find them in the circle of our own acquaintances and neighbors. The slums of many of our cities, into which a "civilized" person will hardly venture to go, can show us places where the Word obviously cannot be heard. But if that everlasting separation from God, which we call hell, is to be the punishment, by what means do those who do not hear deserve this punishment? And if we can speak in terms of fault, does not the fault lie with those who have not carried the Word entrusted to them into these places where it cannot be heard? Or may not the lie with ourselves, when we think of our acquaintances, to whom we have obviously not been convincing enough in our lives and our words to make them ask an honest question about what it is that we claim to live by as believers? Do not all of us know some excellent people among our acquaintances who are unselfish, who live for others, who radiate a warming humanity—and yet Christ is not a subject that seriously concerns them? Where would the fault lie—except with us? Perhaps the "dizziness" of which we spoke is not merely the "theoretical" dizziness which we feel when we are confronted with an overwhelming problem, but rather the dizziness of an existential dread about ourselves and what we have to answer for as messengers of Christ. And we suspect that possibly the questions the judge will ask in the Last Judgment will be quite different from those we set forth in our dogmatic schemes, that perhaps that judge will not simply say, "All who believed in my Son on the right side with the sheep, and all for whom he played no part on the left side with the goats." Most certainly there will be a separation between the sheep and the goats. But possibly the line of separation will fall somewhere altogether different from where we think. Perhaps the first question the eternal judge will ask will be, "Who has known my Word and what has he done with it?" There is a rumbling of this ominous question in Peter's saying that the judgment will begin with the household of God.[2]

It may well be, therefore, that we shall not only receive a completely unexpected answer to our question about the eternal fate of unbelievers, but that on top of this we shall also have to conclude that we have put the question in an altogether *wrong* way. For obviously it is always wrong to ask about others without at the same time including ourselves and our attitude toward them.

The question "Who is my neighbor?"[3] is one that is already on the borderline of what is permissible. For when we ask in this way we are concerned less with the question of the person who is committed to our charge than with the person who is *not* imposed upon us and about whom we do not have to worry at all.

But this question about others is very definitely rejected when I am only theoretically and distantly interested in them, and thus, strictly speaking, am not interested in them at all. Such a question could run like this, for example: "Lord, will those who are saved be few?"[4] It may sound a bit more melodramatic, but probably it is not unfair to the questioners to put the question in a negative form. Then it would run this way: "Lord, will those who are damned be many?" What will be the proportion of the accepted and the rejected in eternity? The answer Jesus gave is exactly in line with what I have just indicated. That is to say, in the strict sense it is not at all an answer to the question as it was asked, but rather a downright correction of the way in which the question is put. It therefore shows that no answer at all can be received so long as the question is put in this way. His answer is a completely unexpected imperative: "Strive"—that is, you who have asked this question!—"to enter by the narrow door."[5] The problem of numbers has been transformed into a problem of which door to enter. And when it is a question of the narrow door it is a question about me. And when my mind is given over to false questions and

[2] I Pet. 4:17.
[3] Luke 10:29.
[4] Luke 13:23.
[5] Luke 13:24.

inept inquisitiveness the door may well become too narrow for me. Suddenly I may find myself standing outside. For I shall get in only if I keep pursuing the true theme of my life.

But this question of the fate of "others" is certainly the wrong theme. I simply cannot ask about the fate of others if it is a question put from a position of uncommitted aloofness and if at the same time I do not confess that I have been sent to them as a messenger.

In my experience, therefore, it was above all a man like Friedrich von Bodelschwingh who legitimately asked this question about the fate of others. When he called for social work among the vagabonds, for missions to the slums (including pagan lands), the main impulse of the beginning of this work was his statement, "Otherwise they will die on our hands over there." And what he meant, of course, was that if they die over there without having heard anything from us about the one hope in life and in death, then their temporal and eternal destiny falls back upon us, who owe to them the redeeming Word.

So Bodelschwingh too asked, "What will happen to them?" But he asked out of commitment, engagement, and in the next moment his question became a commission. The uncommitted, unengaged question, however, becomes a judgment.

I wanted, you may recall, to divide the question asked and consider two sides of the problem. We have now dealt with the first side of the problem. It arose from the observation that a certain number of people have never even heard the crucial question that makes the difference between heaven and hell. This led to the question whether anyone who has never been confronted with the real theme of his life can be called guilty and consigned to condemnation. Here we saw how in the very asking of the question of judgment it is changed and suddenly applies, not to atheists and non-christians, but to those who have failed to do something about it, and therefore to ourselves. Hence we should take care not to ask questions which we have no right to ask. The noncommitted have no right to ask any questions.

The *second* side of the problem presented by our question may be stated as follows. The question of what happens to unbelievers in eternity is understandable—at least theoretically—only on one condition, namely, that we have only a limited time, the time between birth and death, to make our decision for or against God, that this time comes to an end and cannot be altered or prolonged.

This is in fact the view of this decision which is transmitted to us by the New Testament. To see this we have only to look at the parable of the rich man and Lazarus.[6] It is true, of course, that this parable deals with "Abraham's bosom" and "the torments of hell." And yet its aim is not to give us information about the geography of the next world. Its real theme is not the world beyond at all, but rather an extremely this-worldly situation.

When the rich man saw the hopelessness of his everlasting rejection and realized that nothing could be changed, he suddenly remembered his five brothers who were still pursuing their merry journey on earth. But perhaps the word "journey" is putting it a little too strongly, since it always implies that it has a goal and is therefore meaningful and purposeful. But obviously the rich man was afraid that his brothers were missing the goal and paying no attention to the signs at the crossroads. He suspected that instead of pursuing an ordered, purposeful life they were merely "bumming" through life, that they were vegetating rather than existing, without the foggiest notion of what it was all about or of the fact that everything could suddenly and abruptly come to an end, as it had with the rich man himself. And in view of this perilous strolling and reeling through life in which they were in danger of losing everything and flunking every decision, the rich man in hell cried out to Father Abraham: Please send a messenger to give them a firsthand report of what the conditions are here and make it clear to them what kind of crossroads they are facing and what awaits them at the end of either course they take. Then they will believe; then they will recognize the turning points they so ignorantly pass by.

[6] Luke 16:19 ff. For a more extended treatment see *The Waiting Father* (New York: Harper & Row, 1959), pp. 41 ff.

The rich man is therefore not concerned about an account of the next world for its own sake. He wants it as a means to an end, namely, to teach his brothers how important are the crossroads of decision in life.

But Father Abraham replies: It can't be done and it won't work anyhow. They have Moses and the prophets, they have the Word of God. If they will not listen to them, they will not accept a report from the next world either; they will simply dismiss it as occultistic bugaboo. He who does not want to listen will always find reasons to argue away what he hears.

Of course, Father Abraham did not say this in so many words, but I believe this is what he meant. Applied to us it means that we, who are the five brothers of the rich man, have the very program and theme of our life in our hands when the eternal Word and its message is given to us. And now *we* have received the Word. We have it for a limited period of time. Death is the end of the time of decision. It draws the sum of our life and it will not be prolonged. Then faith will see what it has believed and unbelief will be compelled to see what it has not believed. But faith itself will be ended. Nor will the question that summoned us to decision be asked any more. "Just you wait," says the Curé de Torcy in Georges Bernanos' *The Diary of a Country Priest*. "Wait for the first quarter-of-an-hour's silence. Then the Word will be heard of men—not the voice they rejected, which spoke so quietly: 'I am the Way, the Resurrection and the Life'—but a voice from the depths: 'I am the door forever locked, the road which leads nowhere, the lie, the everlasting dark.' "[7]

This parable also runs on the same line of thought that we characterized under our first point. No sooner are we inclined to indulge for a moment in contemplation of the Beyond, to peer with a certain inquisitiveness into the fascinating "showcase" that seems to give us glimpses of Abraham's bosom and the fires of hell, no sooner do we allow ourselves for a moment to be carried

[7] *The Diary of a Country Priest*, tr. by Pamela Morris (Garden City: Image Books, 1954), p. 16. (Trans.)

away by this seeming panorama of the Beyond, than our gaze is forced back to ourselves and we ourselves are made the point at issue. *We* are the ones who stand at the crossroads (whose forks are so important because they end in either heaven or hell); *we* are the five brothers of the rich man. And here again we cannot remain for a moment in the attitude of the spectator, but are immediately held in duty bound and shown that it is we who are involved.

But we would still not have thought our problem through to the end if we did not take note of another question which obviously cannot be subsumed under this argument. When a person asks what is the fate of another, does this necessarily mean that it it motivated *only* by the inquisitiveness of a spectator? I am thinking, for example, of the anxious question of a mother who has suddenly lost her son in an auto accident. She knows, perhaps, that he had been restless in the ferment of maturing, that he refused to have anything to do with the question of eternity and looked elsewhere for his redeemer. Her prayers, perhaps, returned again and again to the plea and the hope that he would again find his way back to the truth which had become the ground of her certitude and peace. Where now would she seek him in eternity? Certainly we would not dismiss that question as idle curiosity, but rather take it as an expression of a love that is concerned and committed.

Here I must tell you of an incident which brought this problem home to me and forced me to think about it. During World War II a young eighteen-year-old private in a tank division wrote to me with regard to a small pamphlet entitled "Where is God?" which I had written for soldiers. He had written to me in flying haste from the battlefield, and the tone of the letter was really quite bitter. Somewhat abbreviated and laundered, the content could be summed up as follows: "Everything you wrote is junk. I have never met God anywhere yet. But I have found tremendous disproof of him in all the horrible things I have seen. It is better to think of God as nonexistent than to accept that he allows such things to happen." Though the letter was rather coarse, it touched me nevertheless, for I sensed in it a disappointed search. So I wrote back to him, trying as well as I could to get him to listen. After this, several letters passed betwen us, but we really got nowhere. Finally, after not hearing from him for several weeks, I received a letter addressed in another hand with his name on it as the sender. Enclosed was a letter from his mother, saying that he had been killed, and also the last letter he had written to me. In the few sentences which it contained he spoke of Nietzsche who impressed him very much. And again he rejected everything I had sought to tell him and proclaim to him. The letter broke off in the middle of a sentence. He was called away by an alarm and was blown to bits by a shell.

Just as the letter was a fragment, so this young life also remained a fragment. And now the mother, who had, of course, read those last lines, put the question to me, "Where shall I seek him in eternity?" Could I have written to her: "This question is improper; you just look after your own soul's salvation"? Certainly that would have been not only unmerciful but also totally unwarranted. For this was not mere inquisitiveness, but love, love that was really concerned. Can such love be left without an answer? But how was I to answer, when the eternal Word itself leaves us without an answer? And even for the purpose of helping, for pastoral reasons, I certainly could not indulge in blind speculations.

At first I thought I would write the mother a letter of consolation which seemed to be the result of my own reflection upon the love of God. I wanted to tell her that we human beings see only a part of the lives of our neighbors and loved ones. We see her boy only in his storm and stress and immaturity. But God sees the whole. He knows what her boy was really doing when he rejected him. He sees the part of his life that was lacking, the lack of which made of it a fragment. He sees the unfinished boy as he would have become.

But then I was still not quite sure that I had really "thought through" the love of God to the end or whether perhaps I had merely "dreamed up" something that only appeared to be so. Do we know and dare we presume to judge whether that boy would have come to faith in the missing part of his life? Was I not in danger of handing out a human-all-too-human consolation? I believe that even pious ideas are forbidden if their purpose is to fill out gaps which God has obviously left open.

But the predicament of this mother would not let me go and finally I believed that I had found an answer, a word which really could not claim to be a solving, releasing word, but which could perhaps help to deliver a person from the torment of that oppressing question.

And this is often the only way that will tide us over the insoluble problems of our faith. It is my opinion, for example, that all the problems which are connected with predestination are fundamentally and theoretically insoluble. And I think we can recognize among the great theologians that they too always come to the place where they stop trying to give a "solution" of the problem and rather point the way to a "deliverance" from the question itself. And in this case the way of "deliverance" from the question is that it makes it clear to us that predestination cannot be posed from the outside as a speculative problem. Then God becomes merely the First Cause and everything is resolved into a cold, soulless law. The question of predestination, however, is one that is raised legitimately only when I am close to the heart of God, that is, when I ask the question as one who believes and is saved: Why was salvation given to *me* and not to others? And when I ask the question that way, not like a philosopher, but from where I am at the heart of God, then it loses its distress. For then I know him to whom I can refer this question, in the certainty that with him and his higher thoughts it will find its solution.

And so it is with this mother's question concerning the eternal destiny of her boy. I finally wrote to her as follows:

"Hans's destiny is an anxiety that troubles your heart. This I can understand, for I too loved him and sought him. And it grieves me that I cannot simply write and say that God loves those whose lives are unfinished, those who are going through storm and stress, and that therefore he has most certainly received him into his paradise. For the sake of truth and your love I dare not lie to you. Nevertheless I can commend you to that love of God, though in a sense that is different from that kind of false assurance. You know the passage in Scripture that says, 'Cast all your anxieties on him, for he cares about you.'[8] The question of Hans's destiny *is* an anxiety for you. So cast it on him! We have the promise that we never cast amiss, but that our anxiety always 'hits home' to him. He feels the impact of it, he catches it, and he takes it seriously. We do not know how he will deal with it or what he will make of it. But we can be utterly sure that it will not fall back to us unchanged so that we will have to go on holding it helplessly in our hands. So let your anxiety rest safely with him. By way of prayer it will have its effect upon Hans—in a way that is hidden from our speculation. It is a comfort that it is hidden from you and that it is now safe in his hands. The greater our cares the more surely we can trust them to him. All cares are only material from which God wants to form our faith and through which he would draw us closer to himself."

So there are no answers to many questions that faith asks, at any rate no answers that can be given in the style of a dogmatic statement: This is the way it is. There are things that can be spoken only in prayer, that can be expressed only as an anxiety which is immediately cast on God. But then, of course, when we look at it this way, there is not a single question which we are *forbidden* to ask. There is no limit to our questioning, because there are no limits to the cares which we can cast on him. Sometimes these cares are handed back to us to be reformulated, as in the case of those who asked (and were concerned) about whether only a few would be saved. But sometimes they remain with God and he accepts them as they are. I believe that this mother's question about Hans's eternal destiny was a question of this kind.

And yet there is one last step that we must take in our thinking

[8] I Pet. 5:7.

through of the question that was asked. It is true, of course, that there is no other way to God except that of paying earnest heed to his call: "Today (today!), when you hear his voice, today, while your life's clock is still running, harden not your hearts." But perhaps God has other ways to come to *us*, ways over which we have no control. Perhaps he has other ways, beyond death and our limited space of time, to come to those who did not hear his call, to those who lived before Christ (for was he not really a "late-comer" in history?), and to the millions who to this day live beyond the sound of his Word. We simply cannot comprehend that that which for *us* is the Word of life should be withdrawn from and become a judgment of condemnation upon those who do not hear it during their earthly life. Is the Saviour who said of himself, "No one comes to the Father, but by me."[9] to become a barricaded door, a judgment, a barrier for the millions in Russia and Asia who do not know him?

When our reflection upon the love of Jesus and his immeasurable compassion leads us to this ultimate agony of thought and our mind is left helpless at the end of its tether, then may someone speak to us these most mysterious words of God: "For you, to whom the word of salvation is spoken, it is true that death is the ultimate limit for your decision, and I will take upon my heart even the last gasping prayer of the dying man when he says, 'God, be merciful to me a sinner!' But for *me*, for the Lord of the living and the dead, there are no limits to the sway of my mercy. And I know how to find even the dead who call upon me—all those who worshiped false gods because they did not know me and are now forsaken by their fetishes and idols, all those who were snatched away in their youth and died unfinished lives; but also the atheists who lost sight of my Word or heard only a distorted caricature of it. There is no end to my mercy; not even death can set limits to it. I can never give up the souls that are lost. My suffering was great and dreadful enough to make amends even for them."

[9] John 14:6.

This, to be sure, is only a word that speaks by way of intimation and parable and points through the message of the New Testament to a mystery that lies at the extreme boundary of what we can dare to say. It tells us that the gospel is spoken even to the inhabitants of the realm of the dead,[10] that Jesus penetrated *even here* with his redeeming, liberating Word. That can be set down as the limit of all that we can say. It lies at the same limit where we are told that today there is still time to hear his voice, that today "Moses and the prophets" are still speaking to us. That limit can be overpassed only by prayer and not with theses. We can cast our anxieties across the border and they will reach the heart of God.

[10] I Pet. 4:6.

VII

Racial Integration and the Christian

THE PROBLEM OF THE POLITICAL ENGAGEMENT
OF THE CHURCH

QUESTION: On your trip through this country it could not have escaped your notice that we find ourselves in a great domestic political crisis. We still do not know whether the dreadful tragedy, which took place in Dallas,[1] may be related to it. But the race question not only occupies our political thinking; it also troubles our conscience. Would you tell us what your position is?

ANSWER: You may well believe that I have not only run into this question everywhere but that it has also been directly presented to me in many discussions. I must first confess what I have been obliged in such cases to say to others in such discussions, and that is how terribly hesitant I feel about expressing myself on this question. On this journey I have often agonized over the question whether I ought not to speak more plainly about this problem and above all to say *more* about it, whether it was not my duty to disturb some all too placid (or seemingly placid) consciences, to give some comfort to many despairing and helpless consciences, and to say something to them which might possibly help them to face the problem. I often had the feeling that in these difficulties people were really looking for a pastor, and I have frequently met with very real desperation and hard personal situations. And sometimes it appeared to me that people were hoping that an outsider would be able to give them some helpful perspective on the matter.

[1] The question was raised in a discussion shortly after the assassination of President Kennedy.

112

But I see myself facing a number of difficulties if I am to talk to you on this problem. And just because I do not want to evade giving an answer simply by saying that I am not competent to do so, I must nevertheless ease my conscience a bit by telling you what these difficulties are.

First and foremost, I come from a country in which the race question was likewise the central point in the saddest chapter of its history. If I wanted to, I could say that I have had my experiences with this problem and therefore do not need to talk about it like a blind man talking about color. My situation, however, is rather that of the burned child who avoids the fire. The way in which we failed to overcome the race problem (which in our case was even worse because it was artificially incited) could simply deprive one of any right to stand up in America and give advice. Naturally the situation in a totalitarian dictatorship was incomparably harder and therefore required a greater degree of courage than would be necessary in this country. Nevertheless the gigantic magnitude of the human tragedy involved should have evoked an extraordinary response and sacrifice. This was ventured, however, only in isolated cases.

So no matter which way I turned, I could not escape my hesitation about saying something about the race question in response to your request without at least stating clearly that I am conscious of my ambiguous situation.

The other difficulty involved in saying something on this question is the fact that I am not an American and therefore speak as an outsider. And that statement leads us directly into the practical problem.

The task of solving the race problem in America is connected not only with the fundamental questions (such as the problem of the image of man, the evaluation of racial differences, etc.); it also has to do with questions of historical development and the irrational factors which have issued from it (e.g., emotional habits, instinctive reactions, and perhaps even subconscious sexual attitudes). And finally in the solution of this question there will also have to be certain politically guided developments, which must not become revolutionary and therefore can proceed only step by step and consequently must take into account a great many historical, psychological, and actually existing factors. Only one who is actually affected and concerned, and never an outsider, can comprehend this exceedingly complicated complex of contributing problems. Only the person affected is therefore empowered to make a decision.

Thus abstract declamations, which it would be very easy for me to make and by which perhaps I could withdraw from the affair, would be of no real help. And they would also be unfair.

This became very clear to me in the heated discussion of the atom bomb which we carried on in Germany. Nothing is easier than simply to say, "I am against the atom bomb." As if anybody were "for" it! The question is, however: What will I do when a great power *has* this weapon? Dare I leave it to that power alone and give the green light to a one-sided, atomically augmented push for power? But if I do *not* want to do this—and as a Christian I cannot wish to do so, since Christians should be more realistically aware than others of the problematical undependability of human nature—then the question is what I should do about it. And implicit in this question is a mass of concrete decisions, which a generalized, wholesale, and abstract atom-pacifism usually shirks.

An abstract declamation that says No on this question reminds me of the foolish remark made by the boy whose father sent him to church to represent the family. When the father asked him what the minister had preached about, the boy answered, "About sin." And being asked further, "What did he say about it?" the boy replied, "He was against it." Now that was an abstract declamation. Who of us is not against sin? But *how* to cope with it, *how* to recognize it in its countless variations and disguises and make one's decisions accordingly—*that* is after all the question.

The problems are always in the particulars. We can always dispose of the general very quickly. And because I am not familiar with the particulars, the details, of the race question, I must impose extreme reserve upon myself. It is not only the outsider in me that feels inhibited but also the theologian in me. That is to say, I am of the opinion that the church (including its ecumenical organizations) has lost very much of the confidence of the public and therefore is often no longer taken seriously, because it has uttered so many general statements, so many abstract, generalized, diluted manifestoes about the situation. The church has, as it were, said that it is "against sin." But this is of no help to the sinner who is caught in the difficulty.

I therefore hesitate to proclaim: I believe that all men are equal before God and that they should also be equal in society. Naturally this is true, and when I make such a statement I am presumably saying something you already know and agree with. But it is utterly commonplace. For with you too the question is: Yes, but what should we do about it here and now? Shall we participate in marches on Washington to demonstrate in favor of integration in government circles? Should we open the white universities to Negroes? Should we allow them to move into our residential areas? Should we accept them in our high schools, colleges, and universities?

What should we do? This is the question of detail, of particulars. The answer to it would have to include many value judgments and situational analyses.

Has this confession of my inhibitions been too long for you? Was it too pretentious of me to paint this "soul-picture" for you? I believe, however, that this is more than a mere maudlin outpouring of a pious soul! I believe rather that here we have touched upon a fundamental problem of ethics. The problem is that our decisions are never merely a matter of having a number of principles but also of always considering the means of putting them into practice. But this cannot be done without examining the situation in which we are acting.[2] And if I am not mistaken, your

[2] On the way in which these statements relate to the radical demands of the Sermon on the Mount see *Theologische Ethik*, Band I.

problems and difficulties with regard to the race question lie precisely at this point. Naturally there are people with whom we cannot discuss these things at all, because they idolatrize the white race and thus on principle there is already a great gulf between us. But I am not talking about these people now. I am rather concerned with those who are uncomfortable about racial segregation and racial prejudice and want to get away from this state of affairs. And for *them* the ethical difficulty lies not in the fact that they do not know what they should think about the race question theologically, but rather in the helplessness with which they face the question of a concrete remedy.

Though it is precisely in this area of the concrete that I feel I am not competent to speak, I may perhaps be able to say something about the *direction* which probably should be taken here. I believe that we could divide this task into two parts and consider first the direction of our thinking and then our action.

First, with regard to our *thinking*, it appears to me that the most important task for the Christian is to "deideologize" the race question and make it what it really is, an ethical and political question. By ideologizing I mean the intellectual process by which one elevates a practical question into a metaphysical question, gives it, so to speak, a sacral charge, and attributes to it a content of significance which it does not possess at all.

This process we find occurring especially frequently in questions which enter deeply into the irrational levels of human behavior. There is in us, for example—in later generations this may possibly be broken down—a kind of instinctive defensive reaction against what is strange, and particularly against what is physically strange. Again and again I noted among very friendly and neighborly people in America a certain defensive dread of what is physically alien (or seemingly alien)—and among both colors of skin, not only among whites. It is precisely this feeling, which comes up from unconscious regions and is therefore so difficult to rationalize, that so easily leads to this vague, muddy ideologizing.

Among these would be, for example, the advocacy of the thesis that the races are fundamentally different. This need not be in such an excessive form as that set forth by the Nazis who spoke of the Jews as being subhuman and thus also were so hideously immune to the idea that they were murdering "human beings." This ideologizing can even be present in the thesis that Negroes are intellectually and culturally primitive and therefore must be relegated to their "proper" social level. Ideologies always have the effect of making us blind to reality and, in this case, of blocking off the sober question whether here we are not confusing cause and effect. Are the Negroes by nature primitive, "so that" at most they attend elementary schools, "so that" they are hardly to be found in the higher professions but are rather bootblacks and other kinds of servants? Or may it not be the other way around, that they have been held down by racial prejudice or political considerations, "so that" there was really nothing left for them but the role of the primitive?

In this matter of the causes of the situation, I have my own very definite ideas. But it is not a question of my imposing *my* opinions upon you. It is much more important that you should take seriously the question itself. In any case, to face the question in sober honesty and to free oneself from the spell of common prejudice would be the first act of deideologizing.

This ideological befogging of the question is especially distressing and depressing when we encounter it among Christians. This I experienced in many parts of Africa where for centuries not a few churches (and ministers and theologians!) have been battering the daylights out of the Bible, and where no fakir's trick of reading things into it or out of it is too silly to use to "prove" from the Word of God that God has assigned to the whites the rulership of the world and to the blacks the role of servants to these pale-faced favorites of God. I have often been in discussions with these people and had to hold on to my collar to keep it from bursting as I witnessed these incredibly nonsensical manipulations. Nevertheless, though in other respects I enjoyed their theological and spiritual confidence (in any case I imagine I did), on this point their minds were absolutely closed.

This again is characteristic of ideologized minds. Because the ideologies do not arise from the sphere of calm, sober argumentation, they cannot be met with arguments. For ideologies have not been *found* as expressions of the truth; they have been *willed* as the expression of a definite interest. People *wanted* a justification to the point where it became a universal prejudice, a collective fantasy, and surrounded them like an ever-thickening atmosphere. Arguments are of no avail here; only exorcism will do the trick. All of this is beyond objective, rational understanding; it can be understood only psychologically—or on the basis of a theological analysis of the human *heart*, from which ever since the Fall more mephitic vapors have arisen than ever did from beneath the tripod of the Delphic oracle.

It would be well therefore to examine this heart of man for the purpose of deideologizing. And it ought to be not the heart of others but our own. In this self-examination we should also not push *too* far the idea of the irrational (such as the racial defensive instinct). Otherwise we might possibly be stupefied by another kind of mythological vapor. Often—it seems to me—it is a matter of obscure irrational forces which to an objective observer sometimes appear to be perfectly evident. I think that *fear*, for example, is one of them. This became especially clear to me in the areas of Africa which I visited. There the whites constitute a relatively small minority. Since they have been there for centuries and have gained great profit from its economic and cultural development, the land has become their home, indeed, the "land of their fathers," to which they cling with all their being. And if a minority is to maintain itself politically, it must be very rigidly consistent and unrelenting, not only in holding on to power, but also in its inner self-assertion. One dare not succumb even to the intellectual attempts to dispute their right to this land by various arguments (e.g., that they are interlopers). They are shaken by the naked fear that in the long run their own exposed position cannot be held, especially as they see the decline of white domination everywhere else. They see the ice floe on which they live cracking and melting more and more. So they set themselves to resist with all the more harshness and determination. They proclaim apartheid because to them it seems the only means of maintaining themselves.

Because fear makes them hard and harsh where in the rest of their life they are not this way at all, they feel compelled to find a permanent justification for what is contrary to their own sense of humanity or to the Christian faith. They never allow this to go to the point of impeaching the Word of God, but rather go at it in just the opposite way: they keep on manipulating it until they actually discover that the Word of God authorizes them to act as they are doing. And so they find nothing wrong in the fact that when a synod meets in the name of Jesus Christ, the two black members must sit in another room when they are having dinner. And when they do this they do not feel they are committing a sin, but simply carrying out a duty.

But anybody who sees a bit deeper immediately recognizes that back of all of this is fear, an altogether understandable political fear of the coming night, and they try to meet it with measures which in reality do not allay the fear but actually intensify it because of the pressure of a bad conscience.

Incidentally, I say all this without the least touch of pharisaism, and I do not know what I myself would think if I lived in Africa. Besides, I was too much shaken by a contradiction which was a sign of that inner distress, namely, the contradiction between the depreciation of the Negro dictated by fear and their personal efforts to treat people of their own "kind" with kindness and patriarchal hospitality.

I imagine, then, that I can also detect this fear and this accumulation of fear and bad conscience in the way in which many people justify and practice racial segregation in this country.

The faster rate of increase in the Negro population, their invasion of white neighborhoods, the depreciation of property values, when this does happen—all this in connection with what arises from the irrational levels, likewise produces fear. To be sure, it is not so elemental as in the areas of Africa which we mentioned, for the whites are still in a considerable majority; nevertheless it is there. And certainly you would not attribute it merely to exaggerated sensitiveness if the observer, the sympathetic observer, not infrequently detects evidences of bad conscience here too.

So it seems to me that the task of "thought" consists in recognizing the *factual* side of the problem, that is, as we said, in de-ideologizing the problem.

I believe that it is now clear that this change of perspective must go through some rather painful stages of self-examination. For ideologizing is always a collective process; one can hardly escape it without this exercise of honesty (inward and outward). Even the person who is opposed to it easily becomes the victim of distorted vision—though in an opposite direction. One could observe it happening to oneself in the Third Reich and it can be seen today in those who have fled from Communist countries to West Germany: even opponents of that system are not fully immune to infection. But how is anybody at all to live soberly in this drunken world if not the Christian who knows what is the true measure of things and who has been relieved of fear, the main obstacle to realistic vision?

To me it is quite clear that such a change of perspective requires time. Legislation alone does not bring about the change. Perhaps it should not even come too far ahead of time, but rather maintain a certain synchronization with the inner history of the people. The acceleration of this inner history is certainly not the least of the tasks which confront the education of youth today. The press and television can also contribute here. What is important, it seems to me, is to *see* the goal toward which we must go. You know better than I do whether and to what extent the passage of new laws (or more loyal enforcement of already existing laws) is called for. But however necessary this might be, more important and more elemental in its significance is the call for what I have termed the new perspective, and not only the call but also real work for its realization.

QUESTION: Very well—but what should we do? I am appealing, you see, to your own framing of the question. I can understand your hesitation with regard to the concrete questions. But even from the point of view which you have just set forth there must be measures or at least some approaches that suggest themselves. You will pardon me; naturally I do not wish to press you. But having gone so far, you surely can go a few steps further; for we certainly cannot wait until our "inner history" has developed to its conclusion. Some of us (and of those who are here today I would even say that all or the great majority) have already reached the point where we have seen through the ideologizing. And this is exactly why we are so troubled. We do not need to be roused from a dream. We are already rubbing our eyes! And now someone has to tell us: Look here, you have to go in such and such a direction! Some of us are already on the way and I would be interested to know whether you approve. Please tell us: What shall we do and where shall we begin?

ANSWER: I think I understand your situation and I appreciate the fact that you expect of me only a word or two about where to begin and not a fully worked out program.

A beginning could be made, it seems to me, by allowing a number of Negro students to enter high schools and colleges hitherto open only to whites. I myself have recently had firsthand contact with an example of this in the South where this has been done in a college which you all know and where these admissions have been very successful.

QUESTION: I know the situation there and I know of a whole series of similar cases. But you will have to remember that here the doors have by no means been simply opened to Negro students, at most the door has only been opened a crack. Those who have been so admitted can be counted on the fingers of one hand. Newspaper reports and sometimes the stories of interested parties often give a completely false impression. Strictly speaking, these are merely "symbolic acts." [We noted many in the hall nodding their heads in agreement.]

ANSWER: So what? What do you have against "symbolic solutions"? If they are a symbol of the fact that one is secretly aware of the remote goal, we can be quite satisfied with such a small symbolic solution. It may possibly be even better than having proceeded in an unorganized way to open the school door for all to flock in as they please. I believe that we must always think in terms of developments and not of instant radical solutions which would only provoke dangerous reactions. The one thing that matters is that the development should not get ahead of us and then force us to do what we do not want to do, but rather that we affirm it and encourage it and in this way control it. It is a dangerous thing merely to go along unwillingly, accepting perhaps angrily what no longer can be stopped. We should be steersmen and not merely passengers on this ship.

When it comes to developments which we want to introduce, it is always a matter of taking the next steps, often very small steps, possibly nothing more than "symbolic acts." What Jesus said about being anxious about tomorrow is entirely appropriate here; what matters is what is committed to us *today*. The Word of God is intended to be a lamp for our feet that lights only the next step in the darkness. The big "programmatic" searchlights that try to light up the road a long way ahead do not count for much in the kingdom of God.

And now I believe that a very great deal can happen in these first small, symbolic steps. We practice living together in small homeopathic doses. We learn to know each other, we can or are compelled to discuss things with each other, we learn at first-hand the other person's feeling about existence, and his understanding of the situation. Countless misunderstandings between individuals and groups result from the fact that we learn about each other only through a third party or the printed word. But everything looks completely different when we face each other eye to eye.

I have learned to know some persons of great humanitarian feeling who obviously did not find it hard to drop bombs from a great height upon people whom they were no longer able to see as individual human beings. This is actually true. Not long ago in this country I became acquainted by chance with a former air force officer whose personality commanded confidence, and almost immediately we found inner contact with each other. I spent a long evening with him and got to know him very well. During the conversation it came out that during World War II he had made repeated attacks upon an antiaircraft station that was manned by sixteen-year-old boys. I knew the flak station very well and also those boys. For despite all the existing regulations they had arranged for me to give them religious instruction once a week. Those wonderful hours near those three guns are still vivid in my memory. One time the attacking dive-bomber had a terrible success. The father of one of the boys who just happened to be visiting the station was killed. The kids—for that's all they were—sent word for me to come, since they were utterly shaken. In all probability the American with whom I was sitting so comfortably was that gunner. And when I told him about what had happened there on the ground and as he looked at me, who had been involved in it, it was as if he had been struck a blow. What had been told in the form of a flier's adventures suddenly became something totally different. All at once persons were looking up where before there were only dark spots. This man was a minister. Those boys there on the ground were bound to him by their common faith; they were his young brothers. And as I knew him now, gay and human as he was, they would have loved him if they had met him. And he too would have surely said to them: "You're grand boys!" But they had never seen one another; they had bombarded one another, and almost exactly twenty years later and several thousand miles away I sat with a man. . . .

Well, I will not go on with the story. Never have I been so

struck by the madness of war. But the point we want to make here is this: How different things and people look when we come into direct contact with them! And to turn the race question into an "existential" problem, that is, a problem which is concerned with *people*, it is not necessary for all to speak with all. It can begin with a few representatives, as is done in the case of these symbolical solutions.

I think that this is where Christians especially are challenged. Even though as a guest I must exercise reserve and not be guilty of tactless criticism, there are some things that lie beyond all courteous custom and which it would be a denial not to mention because of discretion. So, for example, I consider it to be utterly intolerable that such a thing as the following can happen among Christians. I mean the situation in which Negroes who innocently wish to enter a "white" church are turned away by the elders guarding the church doors. I know that these are exceptions—even rare and restricted to certain localities. But they do exist. And I believe also that Christians dare not remain silent where discriminatory curfew laws are enacted which prevent any Negro from appearing on the street, or when a Negro does not know where he can eat or stay overnight while traveling.

All this, I take it, does not occur openly, and presumably there are no laws that legalize such things. But they do happen. Whether they occur frequently or seldom and where they occur, you know better than I. But they do happen.

And here certainly it is the individual Christian who is challenged, the individual who in his place in life meets his neighbor of another color. But I believe that the church as an institution also must not remain silent. As the church of the Word it must break the silence about these things. We can have all kinds of objections to the racial laws in many regions of Africa; but at least such laws are open and clear. You know where you are, and when you discuss these questions you need only to cite the laws. That in America the situation is different on this point distresses me very much just because I love this country. Here there are collective unspoken agreements. People know what the democratic ethos demands and therefore human rights are established on paper. In reality, however, it is often quite otherwise.

Here again is the irrational defense, the collective prejudice which is fed by instinct and historical custom. It is characteristic of this unexamined subconscious mind that none of this is viewed objectively, that it does not appear on paper and in the statutes, but rather smolders in the dark.

This contradiction between what is officially established and what is practiced as an "open secret" is in itself destructive; it is like a worm at the core of democracy. But when this gets into the realm of the church itself it is nothing less than deadly. For then the church is denying its message; it turns its saving Word into an ideology for certain groups and there is no worse denial than that. Then unknowingly it simply confirms the Bolshevistic interpretation of the Word, which says that it is nothing more than an ideological superstructure of bourgeois society.

But downright demonic features of this misunderstanding appear when a person quite calmly thinks he can say that Negroes should certainly be Christians, that they should worship the same Lord as we do, but that they should do so in their churches and *only* in their churches. This surely is not to praise the Lord for his greatness that embraces all the races; it is rather to deny him by refusing to accept members of his Body as our neighbors.

Therefore in my judgment one of the first small steps would be for the church of Christ to do away with racial segregation in its own ranks. This gives us a task which we can perform; this is not some big program which exceeds our ability to fulfill.

QUESTION: You know that what you have presented as a challenge is already taking place in many of our churches. You also know that some of us are ashamed and grieved that these other cases still exist among us. One can only hope that they will become increasingly exceptional.

But may I correct you on one point? Apart from isolated in-

stances, it is probably not true that white congregations would
refuse admittance to Negro worshipers. These cases can arise because as a rule in America the churches are located in a particular
residential area. But since the Negro and white inhabitants generally live together in fairly compact communities, this almost
automatically results in the churches being "Negro" or "white."
Naturally the boundary lines are sometimes fluid, especially where
sociological stratifications are in process of changing and where
the Negro population has infiltrated a previously white neighborhood. But this is only an incidental comment. It seems to show me,
however, that the problem is not at all the question whether Negro
worshipers should be admitted. The really decisive question arises
where one has to make up one's mind whether Negro people
should be allowed to settle in a white neighborhood. You certainly
know that property values fall abruptly as soon as the first Negro
residents appear on a street or district of the city. Hence anybody
who sells his house to a Negro buyer incurs the hatred of his
former neighbors. There is, as it were, a kind of community con-
spiracy among the house owners. What should our attitude be
on this? This is precisely where we ministers are repeatedly confronted with the hardest question of conscience.

ANSWER: I have the unpleasant feeling of exposing myself to the
suspicion of dodging the question when I say that I cannot answer
it categorically. As an outsider it is embarrassing for me to be at
a loss for an answer. There is one thing I can do, however, and
that is to help you at least to find the *questions* one must pass
through in order to make such a decision. The decision itself can
be made only by the person involved. And to a large extent it
will depend on the concrete situation.

To begin with, it is again a question of objectivity; for ideo-
logizations can have a fateful effect upon economic questions too.

First: In order to break through the ideological screen one must
first ask oneself whether the depreciation of property values with
the coming of one Negro family is, so to speak, an economic law,
about which nothing can be done, or whether an entirely differ-

ent explanation may not be possible. You will not regard it as presumptuous of me if I suggest that you examine two other possible explanations. I would not do so if I had not made some observation of my own and engaged in numerous discussions of the subject.

One reason for the fall in property values could possibly be what has been called "block-busting," the clever manipulations of real estate men who know how to extend and foment the initial panic among the white residents in order to produce an exodus of the whites and take over the homes at reduced prices, only to sell them dearly to Negro prospects. I heard a highly educated Negro explain the procedure in this way, giving some rather graphic illustrations.

But even if we leave out the part the real estate dealer may play, even the very idea that the infiltration of Negroes will produce what it usually has elsewhere is sufficient to set off a panicky movement among the whites to sell their properties. The real estate agents could not carry on their possible shady tactics without the help of this panic. This would mean that here again the order of cause and effect may possibly run in the opposite direction from what seems to be the case in the ideological distortion of the situation. In this distortion the causal sequence is this: a Negro moves into a street and then draws all the others after him, so that it is only a matter of time before the last whites move away from that neighborhood. In reality, however, the course of affairs could just as well be this: a Negro moves into a street and all the whites move *out* (in expectation of the supposed influx of Negroes) "so that" now the Negroes move in. Consequently, the real truth of the situation could be that it is not because the Negroes are moving in that the whites are afraid and move out, but rather that the Negroes move in because the whites are afraid.

I cannot help it, but here again I believe that these are not primarily economic and social processes, but simply neuroses. And this is exactly the reason why I believe that here the church has a special obligation. For if this is true, then all this falls within the competence of the church's pastoral care, not only as it admonishes people to practice neighborly love, but also as it summons them to be sober and realistic and passes on our Lord's words "Be not afraid" in every conceivable variation. Perhaps then it will be given to the church here and there to put a stop to that "law" of economic depreciation—and show it up as being not a law at all but only the economic aftereffect of a fever.

Second: In the same way one must very soberly examine whether this aversion to a Negro neighbor is really based only on racial defensive instincts or whether it may not have social and cultural causes. We know that on the average the Negro people, through no fault of their own, do not have anywhere near the same living and cultural standards as the white population. We also know that often those who have rapidly become well-to-do and are able to afford a more expensive house in a good residential area are not always the most likable exemplars of their race—whether white or Negro. Might not the whites be succumbing to a self-delusion if they think they are resisting the moving in of a Negro only for racial reasons when in reality they are averse to having somebody near them who is on a lower social or cultural level?

If this is the case, then one would at least have to show a certain understanding of that attitude. After all, everywhere in the world people want to live in an environment which is somewhat homogeneous socially: a professor does not like to live next door to an upstart who plays cheap records all day long, and a successful engineer finds it unpleasant to live on the edge of the slums.

So if people were to realize very clearly that basically they and their neighbors really desire nothing more than social homogeneity, but on the basis of general and collective prejudice regard the Negro as belonging to a lower social level, then even this sober process would mean a great gain. Then the result could be, for example—once the panic mentioned in point one had been eliminated—that people would at least begin to see the Negro as an individual and a person and not as a mere representative of the collective of his race. I believe that this appeal to sober self-examination falls within the competence of preaching and pastoral care and therefore that proclamation of the Word of God must be operative in the sense of deideologizing people's attitudes.

Third: I cannot judge in what order you must proceed, and therefore whether in breaking down this racial neurosis you should allow it to begin specifically with the problem of where people live. Possibly a more sober view of *this* problem can only result from a breaking down of the whole complex of prejudices and therefore one must exercise a certain patience about these attempts to keep white neighborhoods "pure." On the other hand, one must naturally make up one's mind that these complexes cannot be eliminated merely by education and generalized preaching. (This would take much too long a time; time is pressing— and the Negroes are pressing.) Rather the race problem will always present itself in the form of crises and actual, concrete situations. And the problem of Negroes moving into white neighborhoods is one of these. Therefore the appeal for patience and observance of an order of sequence in these matters cannot mean that we avoid all hot issues. Basically we can never do anything but choose between hot issues.

QUESTION: Do you know the terrible conflicts that ministers can get into on these questions, how many of them have broken with their congregations and been driven out with their families? What shall we do when we have our whole congregation against us on this question? This happens frequently. It is perhaps hard for you to imagine what would happen to a minister who tried to help a Negro move into a "white" street against the will of his neighborhood (and thus largely against the will of his congregation). I hope that hitherto we Americans have given you the impression of being friendly, sociable people. And that is what we are. But on these subjects people can suddenly be changed and become furies. Then woe betide him who falls into their hands!

ANSWER: It is very difficult for me to say anything on that point.
During the Hitler period I simply could not bear to listen to
somebody from a neutral country handing out good advice. Often
I wanted to tell them what Chancellor Bismarck used to say when
his Pomeranian country-squire friends accused him of political
unscrupulousness and opportunism: "You just try working at this
job for once!" As an outsider who will not have to pay the costs
of a definite course of action, but will again be taking off across
the ocean, it may be too easy for me to prescribe just what to do.
So if I venture to say anything at all about it, you should know
that I am distressed by the lack of solidarity which makes talk so
"cheap." I certainly do not want to be so pharisaic as to say, "In
your situation this is what I would do." I do not know if this is
what I would really do at all. As far as reliability of the human
heart is concerned, in the school of God we grow ever more
skeptical, and ever more in need of forgiveness.

I think I understand the difficulty of your situation. It is the
reverse side of a tremendous advantage which American Christians
enjoy over against the structure of the church in Germany. Your
congregations here are by and large so much more active and vital
than many in my country because you do not have a national
church which is tied to the state, because the congregations are
self-sustaining, supporting themselves and their ministers through
their offerings. In this way they are far more basically involved in
the life of worship and the service of God. I envy you your laymen and the extent to which they accept church responsibility.
Sometimes when I see this surging life, which even a superficial
busyness cannot cover up, I feel a lump in my throat when I think
of what it is like at home . . .

But as we said, this vital structure of your church has its other
side. Among us the minister can say what he wishes. As long as he
does not steal any silver spoons or commit notorious adultery,
nobody can call him to account. He can even preach when his
church is absolutely empty and delude himself into thinking that
this is due to his uncompromising preaching which scorns to say

what the people want him to say. Practically speaking, nothing can happen to him. But in this country a lot can happen to him in such cases. A congregation is not pleased when the minister fails, and the congregation dwindles. But sometimes it also will not put up with his saying offensive things which he *must* say to them, if he is to be true to his conscience and his ordination vows. If he raps the knuckles of the hardhearted rich too hard, it can happen that the best contributors leave the church. And then there is no money to buy fine robes for the choir and the church has to get along without the minister who has put his foot in it and the search begins for a preacher with a smoother and more popular disposition.

This can happen to a minister who goes the way of conscience and discernment in the race question. And on this point I have had some moving conversations here with fellow ministers who have been driven out of house and home and church or have been threatened with such expulsion if they opened their mouths again. What could I say to them in their distress? It was not only the understandable anxiety and bitterness over having to leave the work which they loved, but also a real distress of conscience in that they were obliged to ask themselves: Who will follow me? Dare I desert the souls who, after all, were committed to my care? Dare I leave them to a hireling who will keep the pious business going but will smoothly sidestep the *one* point where one must speak out and stand firm? What could I say to these men?

Only because I myself experienced similar situations and on one occasion was expelled—though for other reasons—did I venture to say these two things to them.

First: if it is really a blessing that American congregations are self-responsible and self-sustaining, then one must also accept the burdensome side of this blessing. Then one must be willing to pay for the advantage. Certainly it will not do merely to enjoy the advantages of this institutional structure and then become a dumb dog as soon as the cloven foot appears.

Second: every time has its own way of challenging us to make our confession of faith. And everyone who has entered a profession that involves principles—and that is what we *have* chosen!—must reckon with the fact that his prestige in society can suddenly turn into contempt. The man who wants to eliminate this possibility ought rather to become a dentist. Everybody—Democrats and Republicans, Unitarians and Fundamentalists, white and Negro—has the same fearful respect for him. In the fourth century the confessional situation was concentrated upon certain Christological statements and in the Reformation era upon the doctrine of grace. And I will not be so bold as to assert that these have today become a secure and assured part of the church's doctrine. God forbid that I should assert this. It is not assured at all; actually the structure is creaking. And often when I listen to a sermon I imagine how high the fagots would once have been piled for the declaimer of such ideas. But our quite justified aversion to burnings at the stake should not cause us to forget that behind these false measures was an earnest concern for doctrine which we are seriously lacking today.

And yet there is no doubt that the central emphasis of the confession which is laid upon *us* lies precisely in the *ethical attitudes* which are inherent in our faith. Anybody who acts against his conscience in the race question is not only denying the ethical implication of his faith; he is denying the faith itself. It is at these points that we must declare ourselves Christians today. During the Third Reich I once heard that a bishop said, "If Hitler attacks the Augsburg Confession, I will go to the stake." He was a brave man and I trust that he would have done so. But Hitler never attacked the Augsburg Confession. He could not very well do so, since he probably did not know that it even existed. But he did murder the mentally ill and the Jews and he did this in the name of a mad delusion which he constructed out of his idea of the superiority of the Nordic race. That was the hour in which the church of Christ was called to make its confession (and in which, unfortunately, only a few of its members did declare themselves). This was a time that called for the required act of love for one's neighbor and also for resistance to a disastrous false doctrine, namely, a doctrine of man which operated only with biological categories and gave no hint whatsoever that man has been bought with a price and is the apple of God's eye. In the preaching and the action with which a man would have reacted to that act of sabotage against man the gospel itself would have sounded forth in concentrated and actualized form. Here was a theme which would have allowed all its glories to flash and sparkle with light. He who remained silent at this point remained silent altogether. For whatever else he said about Christ would have been mere "blah" which would have been interpreted as routine dogmatic talk, not to be taken seriously. Only when a man is utterly serious and then takes his stand will he be taken seriously. But if he loses his credibility at this point, he can no longer persuade anybody to believe. He can sing hymns and celebrate liturgies and they will be only a noise which is a vexation to God.[3] Today the question appears to present us with a similar *status confessionis*, a situation where we must confess our faith.

To be in a *status confessionis*, however, does not mean that we simply rush in and blindly declare our faith and act recklessly. We should not wish to go faster than God's pace. We must encourage and foster and let the seed grow. And we know where to find forgiveness when we do something wrong or when we try to cover up our failure to act as the gospel requires by saying that we are just letting things grow.

QUESTION: As you know, not long ago there was a gigantic demonstration march on Washington, made up of people from all over the country, the purpose of which was to lend emphasis to the demand for equal civil rights for Negroes. In connection with this there was also a great deal of excitement in many churches, especially in cases where ministers sought to persuade members of their congregations to participate in the demonstration and in some cases went to the demonstration by themselves. This quite fre-

[3] Amos 5:23.

quently led to conflict of the ministers with their congregations or at any rate with large segments of their congregations, and also to vehement theological discussions among the ministers themselves. The conflicts in the congregations were based—just as you have said—upon a differing position with regard to the race question, that is to say, a negative or at least reserved attitude toward the social integration of the Negro. What needs to be said on this question has been said. But I would be interested to know what you would say about the theological discussion among the ministers themselves. The problem at issue was the following:

The Washington demonstration was an attempt to exert pressure on our government and our legislative bodies. It was therefore very emphatically a *political* action. But if the church and its representatives take part in political measures, are they not trespassing where they have no business to be? Dare the church do anything else but express itself on this question in its *preaching and its prayers?* This question was sharpened by the fact that a very well-known churchman took part in these demonstrations. The question can be sharpened even further by putting it this way: Dare the church do anything against the laws of the state? For such demonstrative forms of exerting pressure are contrary to the laws. For us Americans a conflict of the church with the laws of the state is a monstrous conception.

QUESTION FROM THE AUDIENCE: If you say that the church can express itself on the race question only in preaching and in prayer, what does it have to preach and for what shall it pray?
ANSWER OF THE FIRST QUESTIONER: In its preaching it would have to speak of the equality of all men and specifically mention our society's sins against this principle. And it would have to pray for the awakening of men's consciences and for those who have been wronged.

QUESTION FROM THE AUDIENCE: Very well, there can be no doubt that it must do this. But is not more than that involved? When I stand up for the equality of all men on the basis of the Word of God and when I also see that the first condition for its realization consists in the passing of certain laws, must I not then draw the conclusion and demand the passage of such laws with every available means? And if I see that the responsible authorities are being unfairly reluctant, must I not also *demonstrate*, that is, exercise political pressure to accelerate action?

ANSWER OF THE QUESTIONER: I do not deny that this necessity can exist. Nor do I deny that laymen (those who are not in the ministry of preaching and to that extent are not direct representatives of the church) may draw from this preaching the conclusion that such political pressure must be exerted and that they may say: We can exercise our Christian obedience only by going out as Christian citizens and realizing what the message demands of us. I do deny, however, that the church *itself* must draw this conclusion. It simply dare not enter the political arena; its job is simply to furnish the Christian principles for those whose business it is to be concerned with politics [thus not only the professional politician but also the citizen].

FURTHER QUESTION FROM THE AUDIENCE: I do not understand this distinction. The ministers, the officebearers of the church, are, after all, citizens too. Why should they, of all people, be the ones to renounce their civic duties and leave them to the so-called man of the world? I am afraid that here a line of separation is being drawn between the sacred and the profane and that what is being advocated is a schizophrenia of the mind which at any rate is completely alien to Reformation theology.

ANSWER OF THE QUESTIONER: Naturally, I am by no means advocating such a separation. What is involved here is only a difference of functions and duties which must not be confused. [A conflict of opinion became apparent in the audience which indicated approval and disapproval of what had been said.]

THE AUTHOR'S REPLY: Perhaps I may make a comment on this conflict of opinion. Apart from all the concrete questions, the demonstration in Washington obviously had one good thing about it anyway, and that is that it forced people to concern themselves with some fundamental theological questions. I would say that the last few minutes of the discussion have been consciously or unconsciously revolving about Luther's doctrine of the "two kingdoms." Moreover, unlike other theologians, I am of the opinion that it was by no means only Luther who saw this problem, but rather that it appears in every theological ethics, including Catholic and Calvinistic ethics.[4] I do not propose here to give you an outline lecture on this doctrine of the spiritual and the worldly. Rather I shall allow only the outline of it to show through as I indicate something of its application to our problem. Permit me to make three points.

First, when the previous speaker pleads that the church must be slow to enter politics I must defend him against the accusation that he is advocating a kind of schizophrenia and declaring himself in favor of an improper separation between the sacred and the profane. He undoubtedly upheld the proposition that the church should exercise reserve with regard to politics for quite a different reason, and certainly it was not at all his intention to deny a minister of the church the right to have very decided political opinions and therefore the right to be a citizen in the full sense of the word. He certainly did not wish the church and its representatives to be political neuters.

It is a totally different question, however, whether he should set forth his political opinions from the *pulpit* and whether—to use a rather violent metaphor—he should put his pulpit on wheels and shove it ahead of him in a political demonstration march. In other words, the question is not whether he must exercise discipline with regard to politics in the area of his *preaching*. Let me illustrate this question with an example which lies beyond this particular difference of opinion and which comes out of the situation of my own country.

There is no doubt that God does not want war and that war is

[4] Cf. *Theologische Ethik*, Band I.

a sign of the fallen world. Hence there is also no doubt that the church must speak for peace and preach love instead of force. Naturally this question also has its political side, for it confronts one with the task of examining what means should be used to preserve peace and prevent war. The appropriate means, however, are a matter of judgment and opinion. The political reason is qualified to make this judgment. But in one person this political reason may lead to this opinion and in another person to a different judgment. Thus parties holding quite different opinions can develop. Or already existing parties can arrive at different judgments on the basis of their programmatic presuppositions—naturally not only on the question of war but also on almost every concrete particular question in the economic, social, and cultural area. Which political means must I regard as best suited to prevent war, that is, war with modern means of mass extermination? The means of complete disarmament? Or the means of armament with atomic weapons in order to achieve a balance of deterrence and thus a *pax atomica?* In my country these questions have been discussed with great passion and the voices of the theologians were perhaps the most vigorous. On all sides appeal was made to the will of God and to the conscience which recognizes that it is bound by this will of God.

This is where the question whether there can ever be a clear-cut position of the church in such matters of practical judgment becomes very urgent. Since such matters of judgment have to do with reason, and often only with political instinct, it is in fact impossible for a synod of the church to arrive at a unanimous decision on this level of a problem. We have all had plenty of experience with this. What most of such statements amount to is that the church emphasizes its unity in principle (say, on the question of peace and opposition to war, the affirmation of human rights, or the sanctity of marriage), but that it must confess that there are divergent judgments on the question of *how* these principles are to be realized here and now. There is no consensus on the assessment of the situation, the political prognoses, and the choice of the proper means. The accumulated political wisdom of the democracies has given expression to this insight in the fact that they regard parties as being the basic means by which they function.

Now my rhetorical question would be this: Does not the demand that the church exercise reserve in political matters look quite different from this point of view? The church exists for everybody, for Democrats and Republicans, for employers and employees, for the rich and the poor. All of these will take different positions on a particular question. And it is illegitimate for the church to make itself the advocate of any special interest group. Precisely because the minister must realize that—from a social and political point of view—as an individual he represents a partial, one-sided interest, he must never allow his personal position in the conflict of opinion, in the struggle of interests, and also within the social structure to constitute any limitation whatsoever upon the fact that his spiritual "authority" is for all. His task (and he should be content with it, for fundamentally it is a very great one!) is to proclaim the commandments of God and thus the principles of our thought and action. His task is, so to speak, to keep the compass set correctly. And now we have to go out into the country with this compass which we have received. When the compass points to the southwest this does not mean that we must stubbornly head straight in this direction, through rivers, mountains, and deserts. This would be foolish and fanatical. Rather, *while* keeping our eye on the right direction, we must take into account the nature of the terrain and seek out the best bridges over the rivers and the best paths over the mountains and through the deserts, in order to hold to the direction of the compass under the given conditions and within the context of the available means.

The doctrine of the two kingdoms in all its various forms seeks to deal with precisely this problem, namely, the question of how we can fulfill the commandment of God in the framework of the laws and conditions of this aeon. As Christians we have the same compass and the same compass setting. But the choice of political, economic, and social roads will be made differently, simply because our judgments concerning the terrain are different. It is true that as preachers of the gospel we must set the compass, but we are not leaders in the political terrain. If, contrary to our commission, we insist upon doing so nevertheless, we break the *communio viatorum*, the community of pilgrims, into various groups which split apart, not upon a difference of decision with regard to the gospel, but rather upon a difference of highly secular opinion. Then we are arbitrarily dismembering the body of Christ.

I would think, then, that it is not necessary for me now to apply this in detail to the race problem in America. The "setting" of the compass would mean that we proclaim the rights of our Negro neighbor and that we not only demand that these rights be guaranteed by law but also speak plainly about the injustices that are done to him under the shadow of existing laws and also outside the law. But above all it is a matter of preaching the gospel in such a way that these implications become perfectly evident, even though they are not dealt with explicitly every Sunday (*this* we certainly ought not to do!). Then the *march* with this compass (as distinguished from the *setting* of the compass) would require that those who listen to us seek, within the scope of their competence and ability, ways in the political terrain which are in keeping with the compass setting. The march on Washington could well have been in line with this.

Second, related to this is the fact that the church dare not assert itself as an independent power within the political power struggle in order to carry out its own so-called will, but must rather suffer in the name of the gospel and ally itself in solidarity with the sufferers. I can illustrate what I mean with a remark which Luther made—I think in his *Table-talk*. There he said something like this: Suppose that I am walking through a forest and am set upon by a robber. I would then defend myself and even be prepared if necessary to dispatch him in order to protect myself. In such a moment I am something like an acting or delegated government which is appointed by God to combat murder and chaos. But suppose I am taking the sacrament to a dying man and, going through the same forest, I am attacked by a man who wants to kill me out of hatred for Christ. Then I could not defend myself, but would have to let myself be killed; for in this case I am a representative of the church of Jesus Christ which must suffer for the sake of the gospel and dare not assert itself by means of force. To be sure, Luther would have something to say to the one who attacks him because of the gospel and would seek to waken his conscience; but he would not have recourse to the means of force.

It seems to me that the church is in an analogous situation in overcoming the race problem. It has to take its stand with the insulted and injured and take upon itself the suffering (the contempt and opposition) that then comes to it. It certainly has something to say to the society and the state which acts in this way. But it is not its office to bring itself into play as a political force.

Naturally faithfulness to the gospel—particularly at points which have such great political relevance—will in itself represent a certain *political* potency. A church which is faithful to its mission will always be *also* a "moral" force and to that extent it will also be an indirect political factor. This will be, as it were, "added unto it" and this it can count upon. But this can never be its real and certainly not its sole goal.

QUESTION: But are there not cases, perhaps boundary-line cases, in which the need is so enormous that the church must address itself directly to the matter and possibly even intervene in a massive way?

ANSWER: I was just about to speak of this boundary-line situation.

Third, if it is a question of my neighbor's ultimate destiny, perhaps of his life or death, and there is nobody who will stand up for him, then the church may be called upon to be an emergency deputy for the society or the state which is derelict to its duty.

I may mention two examples of this boundary-line situation, taken from my own immediate experience, which show the basic outlines of our problem.

During the time of famine and catastrophe after World War II, Eugen Gerstenmaier, the current president of the Lower House of the German Parliament, organized and built up a gigantic church relief organization (*Hilfswerk*). I know him well and was rather close to this whole development. At the outset this relief organization asked fellow believers in other countries for contributions. Especially from America tremendously great quantities of gifts in kind were sent over—food, clothing, and many other things. (Gratitude for the help that was given in that hour and by a former "enemy" has not yet been erased from our hearts.) After a time somebody came upon the idea that the contributions might be made even more valuable and productive if raw materials rather than finished goods were requested. It would be possible to buy larger quantities of materials for the same amount of money by saving the cost of American manufacturing and wages. Thus it would be possible with this material to reactivate idle factories in Germany and thus revive our industry which had been crippled. I am purposely simplifying the procedure somewhat in order that we may not spend too much time on it.

But when this procedure was followed the church thus undertook to perform business and industrial tasks; this meant that it had to co-operate with factories and concerns and enter actively into some very complicated economic operations. Moreover, it was unavoidable that the church thus engaged had also to assume enormous financial risks, as is inevitable in a free economy. Gerstenmaier became, as it were, the general manager of a mammoth corporation in which the church occupied a key position by way of the *Hilfswerk*.

I still remember very clearly a number of discussions in which leading churchmen tried to stop this rather sweeping development by furiously waving a red light. When they used theological language, they said: "This is confusing the two kingdoms. The church is assuming economic tasks which do not belong to it. It is becoming a great industrialist instead of preaching to the industrialists." It was also possible to say with a defensive instinct

which had been much less thought through theologically: "Where
will we end up if this kind of thing goes on? Aren't we heading
straight for an economic theocracy? And if the thing fails, if this
mammoth concern goes bankrupt (and with ministers as general
managers this is quite in the cards!), the church will not only turn
suddenly into a poor Lazarus with empty pockets but will also
suffer a tremendous loss of prestige. And the children of this
world, who, as is well known, are wiser than the children of light,
will again be able to say with glee, 'Shoemaker, stick to your
last!' "

And I also know exactly what Gerstenmaier's reply was to this
reproach. He flushed with anger, perhaps precisely because he is
a good theologian and would not like to be accused of having
overlooked so fundamental a doctrine as that of the two kingdoms.
He said, "Naturally I know all that you have been saying. Naturally the church 'should' not be in business, should not be a great
industrialist. But what if at this moment—in the midst of this postwar chaos—there is nobody else but the church who can tackle
this in a big way? What if at this moment it is the only big
corporation which is still fairly intact, which sees the need and
can step into the breach? Should it then say: I will overstep my
bounds if I give help? For one thing is sure: if I were to close up
the *Hilfswerk* today, even by tomorrow thousands would die of
hunger and freeze to death in their unheated rooms and without
any protecting clothing—old people and children above all. They
would be lying dead in our streets!"

This, you see, was a case in which the church was really called
upon to act as a kind of deputy of society and the state. If we
think of analogies in the life of the state we can think of exceptional situations which are called forth by national emergencies.

If the distress of my Negro neighbor became intolerable and I
saw that—despite all the preaching of the church—nothing whatsoever happened so far as the state and society were concerned,
that the status quo was stubbornly maintained, then I believe that
in America too the hour would come in which the churches of

this country could be called into this emergency situation where they would really have to take hold as a "power in public life" and do some kind of organizing. On several occasions in this country I was assured that that time had come at the Washington demonstration. Others told me that it was really time for that to happen in this local situation. It cannot be my task to judge whether this is so. All I can do is to indicate the fundamental outlines of such a boundary-line situation in order to manifest a *possibility*.

And now the second example. When Hitler carried through his murderous assault upon the Jews and the mentally defective, there was not in that Germany which had been co-ordinated from top to bottom a single institution which was free enough to make a public protest. Only the churches could do so—or must I say, they could have done so? The church was the one voice that could make the cry of the tormented to be heard and furnish it with the commentary of the preaching of judgment. There were some brave men of both confessions—I am thinking above all of Bishop Wurm of Württemberg and Count von Galen, the Catholic Bishop of Münster—who did raise their voices. Certainly it would have been well, and surely it was called for, if Christianity in Germany had spoken with one determined, unanimous voice in this situation. But this is not what we are discussing here. If there was at this point a possibility for the church, not only through its public preaching, but also through direct exertion of power (by strengthening resistance groups, mobilizing Christians outside of Germany), to save human beings from death and put a stop to this crime, then I would consider this too a genuine situation in which the church should step in where the government had failed and incriminated itself.

Unfortunately I must speak here in unreal terms, for I know that the total ideological dictatorship would have killed every attempt of this kind before it was born. But the point I want to make here is not what would have been *possible* in a particular historical *situation*, but rather to present a model case which would illustrate the situation in which the church may become an emergency substitute for society and the state. And again I must ask you to apply the outline to your own situation.

QUESTION: May I come back once more to the "normal situation" in which we apparently find ourselves, that is, the situation in which we are not yet confronted with the boundary-line case of the church having to act in an emergency. I ask myself whether even in the context of this "normal situation" the church can be content only with its preaching. I believe that many forces in our society will have to work together to solve the race question in a constructive and positive way.

ANSWER: There you are certainly right. It would be an evidence of poverty, which I would surely not expect to be the case, if the church were the only force in this country which would proceed along the lines we have indicated in facing the race question. But to me it does seem important that the church should have its influence upon its actual and potential allies.

To my great joy I have noted in America some beginnings of a movement toward the formation of "evangelical academies," which have been so fruitful among us. Here, for example, there could be a place where the church could speak with the responsible people in all areas—politicians, teachers, welfare workers and administrators, and many others. And here or in other places . . . well, now I must say something for which I must accept responsibility as being my own opinion. This may surprise you very much, but I do not mean it as a joke at all. I think I have discovered in America a secret new religion. It is the worship of psychology. I believe that its priests in this country have almost unprecedented power and enjoy an almost unlimited prestige. Is there really any problem in life, large or picayune, with which people do not run to the psychiatrist or psychotherapist? I even have the feeling (you will pardon me if this sounds somewhat malicious) that many people do this merely out of boredom, because they get some kind of kick out of it, or because of an introverted interest in themselves. I regard this new cult as a very great danger and I think that the position which is accorded to the psycho-strategists and psycho-tacticians represents a great temptation to them (incidentally in a financial respect too). Now I have askęd many people, especially the "initiate," whether American psychologists have also addressed themselves to the race question. I would be very much interested in such investigations. I would like to know, for example, what lies behind the neuroses we have been talking about, whether it is a question, for example, of a subconscious sexual problem or something else. In these interviews I have never found an answer. Naturally, it is possible that I was always talking to the wrong people, though this would seem to be very strange. In any case, not much seems to be available in this area; otherwise word of it would surely have gotten around.

How would it be if the psychologists were diverted a bit from hypertrophic preoccupation with individual cases and encouraged to make a psychological study of the race problem? Perhaps they could do some fruitful work on this very fundamental question. (Surely no one will interpret what I say as being a wholesale disparagement of all work with individual cases. This, of course, would be utterly foolish.) I believe that something like a collective psychotherapy with respect to the race question would not be the least of what we should wish for. To stimulate something like this could also be a part of the search for helps and helpers which the church should be pursuing. Political and civic groups might also have an interest in this; for the subconscious, especially when it exhibits a collective "bad conscience," can in the next act become a destructive political force.

In any case, however, I do not have the impression that I have really been able to give you a "solution" of the problem. The more I reflect upon it the more immense it becomes. The only purpose of very modest endeavor has been to call attention to several wrong attitudes (especially the ideologization of the problem). Even the elimination of these attitudes, however, would not of itself solve the problem. And I know that despite our very real concern, many questions have not even been mentioned.

VIII

The Nazi Regime

AN INTERPRETATION OF RECENT GERMAN HISTORY

QUESTION: I expect that during your visit you have frequently been asked how the terrible things perpetrated by Hitler could ever have happened in a country which brought forth Bach, Beethoven, Thomas Mann and other luminaries of art and science. I too would like to present this question. There are many friends of Germany in this country. We admire the way in which your country has recovered after the catastrophe, and German theology also has great influence in this country. But for this very reason we simply do not know how to explain and reconcile this combination of greatness and cruel criminality. Moreover, as everywhere else, there are many in this room who are of German background, and they especially are troubled by this question.

ANSWER: This question does indeed seem to trouble many Americans and has often been put to me; I am rather afraid of it, but not really because it is a "hot" subject. (I have grown somewhat inured to "hot" questions!) I am afraid of it rather because it involves such a tremendous complex of political, historical, and psychological problems. When one has directly participated in that phase of history, when one's own life and lot were affected by it, and one has had constantly to preach the Word of God and address it to that situation, one would naturally have reflected a great deal about it and also talked to countless people about it. Consider what it meant to have to speak week after week during the bombing raids to people, some of whom had lost everything and were living in panic fear of the next night; to soldiers home

146

on brief leave from the front; to Gestapo people in repeated
interrogations, and later, when the Americans admitted me to the
detention camp for imprisoned government personnel, SS leaders,
and generals; to the people responsible for that epoch who were
experiencing, at the very nadir of utter failure, a dreadful (or
fruitful) hour of reflection. So I have had to regard and ponder
that historical epoch from an unusual number of points of view.
There was only *one* characteristic that was common to all of these
points of view: it was always a view that came out of direct in-
volvement and engagement. I talked with rabid Nazis, but also
with men and women of the Resistance (not a few of whom were
later murdered); with former Nazis whose eyes had been opened
and were now going through terrible torments of conscience; with
soldiers who thought they were fighting at the front for their
fatherland and whose fathers (some of them pastors of the Confessing Church) had been thrown into prison by the rulers of this
very fatherland (you can imagine the conflict that these young
men were going through); with people in terror during the nights
of bombing; with mothers and wives who had lost their dearest
on the battlefields, not knowing for whom they were making this
sacrifice, for their fatherland or for a criminal; with young SS men
who realized whose wagon it was they were hitched to and asked
me what they should do; with a dying man who threw his hot
water bottle at the crucifix.

Believe me, I encountered all the shades and refractions of the
sulphurous light of that epoch. And naturally this way of viewing
the situation is quite different from what it is for you who look at
it from a geographical and political distance. Even with all the
powers of imagination, a citizen of a free constitutional state
probably cannot visualize what happens in an ideological tyranny,
what happens to a people that—to borrow a metaphor from some
of Goethe's verses—is dragged over half the earth by a cruel con-
queror and then is carried along into the same abyss into which
he plunges.

But the more I have thought about these events in the past years and also studied the abundant literature on the subject the more obscure and puzzling it has all become. So I can only hope to show you a small part of this complex problem. The far greater part of this historical iceberg, however, will remain beneath the surface.

But above all I must confess that the form of your question confronts me with a real difficulty. For you ask me how all this was possible among a people to whom the world owes no inconsiderable part of intellectual and moral heritage. In other words, you are asking *how* it could have happened. The ideal answer to that question would consist in my being able to show you an exact causal nexus and then point to an inevitable unrolling of a historical process. But this I not only *cannot* do but should not even *want* to do. For if I *wanted* to do this, it would mean that I wanted to deny all historical guilt, that I would be trying to "deduce" it logically and thus turn it into an amoral fate. If I were to interpret the Nazi regime and its horror as the necessary outworking of natural law, I would be turning history into nature. This would be a vicious manipulation, and I would certainly have a bad conscience if one of you were to fall into this trap and at the end of my presentation would say: The Germans are not guilty of what the Nazis did; it "couldn't" have been otherwise; they were the victims of fate.

So when I say something about the question of "how" this could have happened, I do not mean this as in any sense an "excuse" which takes flight into an illicit amoral realm beyond good and evil. This is what I have tried to make clear in this rather theoretical sounding introduction. My only purpose in making these comments, however, had been to help you to "understand" these events (which is, of course, quite different from "explaining" them![1]) Only so, it seems to me, could I get across to you what I am really concerned about, namely, that you cannot look at what happened in Germany from a distance, like a disinterested specta-

[1] Wilhelm Dilthey and Karl Jaspers have worked out the philosophical implications of this fundamental difference between "understanding" (which relates to historical personal life) and "explanation" (which deals with the scientific process of cause and effect).

tor viewing a spectacle of nature, but rather that here we are
confronted with an excess of subhumanity which is potentially
present *wherever* there are human beings. This potentiality is
present in America too. Here too, as Nietzsche said, the "thin film
over the boiling lava" can burst one day and bring to light abysses
which no comfortable, self-confident citizen has ever dared to
reckon with.

So I want to say a few things (obviously far too few!) for the
sake of "understanding" and select from all that should be said
what seems likely to create that understanding.

Allow me first to give a sketchy characterization of the factors
which were operative as a "precondition" (not as a "cause"!).

First: The so-called "Weimar State," which Hitler then so hor-
ribly liquidated, left the German people in a desperate situation. A
host of many millions of unemployed crippled an economy which
was already gasping for breath. But one ought not to speak only of
the economy itself, but rather above all to visualize the psychological situation of its victims, the unemployed, their complaints that
they and their families were living below the level of subsistence,
that they were having to lead a meaningless bare existence at the
cost of others and having to stand day after day in long queues to
get a certification of unemployment; that they lived in a constant
atmosphere of a collective discontent which always breeds in such
situations.

Second: The fragmentation of the state into almost innumerable
parties, the state's complete lack of any symbolic power to fire
the imagination, the rapid succession of governments, none of
which was able to produce an authoritative representative of
deeper ties or radiate any confidence among all the fragmented
groups—all this inevitably fostered the disastrous feeling of hopelessness.

Third: Along with this one must not forget the extent to which
the Versailles peace treaty after World War I contributed to this
material and psychological paralysis. The occupied zones of Germany suffered severely and this inevitably generated a nationalism

(including champions of it in the form of highly fanatical *groups*) that not only was turned against the state, which was regarded as impotent, but also had in it elements which were partly reactionary (mourning over the lost imperial glory) and partly revolutionary (pressing for a dictatorship). It is certain that through the terrible folly of that treaty the victors contributed not a little to the generation of a collective despair and hopelessness, which eventuated in an explosion, the cry for a strong man, and the willingness to worship this false savior uncritically if only he could turn stones into bread and leap unharmed from the pinnacle of the temple.

I have intentionally alluded to the scene of the temptation in the desert in order to indicate that what was brewing here bore the marks of the demonic. There is a degree of despair and misery in which people do not care who liberates them from darkness and ruin or how illusory is the light to which they are being led.

So when I plead for an "understanding" of these events, this does not mean that I am shutting my eyes to the question of guilt. (I speak of the demonic character of the situation only to emphasize this, not to cover it up.) For naturally it is a sin to be indifferent to the question of who it is one sells oneself to, hide and hair—though the matter is made more complicated by the fact that the pseudo-savior can disguise his hide and hair (which Hitler actually did). And it is also a sin to allow oneself later to be blinded by the glitter of unexampled success in the economic, social, and political realm; it is a sin to regard with utter amazement and delight the sum of these achievements and in the process forget in whose name and at what terrible cost of iniquity these accomplishments were achieved.

But just because I see the sin and the guilt in this way, I am afraid of the pharisaical feelings which such a "confession" could provoke, and therefore I immediately ask: Who dares to cast the first stone? Who does not live in a glass house? Who would assert that he would be immune to such temptations in such a situation? When we Germans speak of guilt and sin in this matter, then we must confess it to *God*. We would also have to confess it before those who can no longer hear that confession, before those who were gassed and cruelly murdered. But I have inhibitions about regarding just anybody as a potential father-confessor—just anybody who is perhaps not at all in a position to hear that confession in solidarity before God and is therefore all the more likely to fall into the position of turning the confessor's seat into the seat of the Pharisee instead of seeing that it is a "glass house." Therefore I have never had much regard for collective confessions of sin before all the world, and after the war I made not a few enemies by openly proclaiming these inhibitions.

But here I have already become involved in comments; let me rather continue with the enumeration of the historical facts.

Fourth: So people clamored for the strong man, the apocalyptic redeemer-figure, and were content to stake everything on this last card. And lo, the figure offered itself in Hitler. And it offered itself in a very subtle and cunning way. And this again suggests the analogy to the demonic, the style of the satanic gesture by which the diabolical adversary disguises himself as an "angel of light."

Hitler knew how to dissemble and one had to look very closely and read his terrible book *Mein Kampf* very carefully to see the cloven hoof beneath the angel's luminous robes. He made free use of the Christian vocabulary, talked about the blessing of the Almighty and the Christian confessions which would become the pillars of the new state, he rang bells and pulled out all the organ stops. He assumed the earnestness of a man who is utterly weighed down by historic responsibility. He handed out pious stories to the press, especially the church papers. It was reported, for example, that he showed his tattered Bible to some deaconesses and declared that he drew the strength for his great work from the Word of God. He was able to introduce a pietistic timbre into his voice which caused many religious people to welcome him as a man sent from God. And a skillful propaganda machine saw to it that despite all the atrocities which were already occurring and despite the rabid invasions of the Nazis in the churches, the rumor got around that the good Führer knew nothing about these things. (Whether we really did not know that the good Führer knew it after all is another question). By the time when people gradually found out who the central figure really was and that the other members of the firm were well suited to him ("Jack is as good as his master," we say in German), the master was already secure in the saddle and judging by human standards there was nothing that could be done about it. Then the size of the firm grew larger than ever; and one can imagine what happens when the dregs of a people come to the top, when people who in normal life would never have amounted to anything, secure positions both petty and powerful.

The few idealists who were involved in the movement soon went down. Besides, from a certain point on, idealism is in itself a real delusion. As the bitter folk humor expressed it at that time, of the three qualities, namely, being a Nazi, being intelligent, and having character, one can have only two. Either one can be a Nazi and be intelligent, in which case one has no character; or one can be a Nazi and have character, in which case one is not intelligent; or one can be intelligent and have character, in which case one is not a Nazi.

Fifth: All this raises the question why people did not rise up against Hitler when they began to see what a prince of the underworld he was.

The answer to that must first deal with the question *who* found him out at all. This process of finding out the truth went on only very gradually and even then it was only partial. It happened only to the extent to which one came in touch with the terror and the massive injustice in one's personal life or in the radius of one's own experience. Good care was taken that one should not see this happening to others. It either did not appear in the newspapers at all or in such a way that the readers (or those who listened to the speeches) were subjected by means of inflammatory accounts to the suggestion that the terrorist measures were simply retaliatory justice. When day after day for years there was nothing but talk

of the crimes of the Jews, when one could read nothing but ficti-
tious "documentary" accounts of Jewish owners of houses of
prostitution, mass profiteering, exploitations, wars, and the multi-
plication of armaments, when the image of the Jews was obtained
almost solely from caricatures and pornographic political newspapers,[2] it required a very considerable inner substance, insight,
and objectivity to arm oneself against it. Perhaps, then, one can
understand that naïve people (and how many such there are all
around us!) would say what I heard said any number of times: "I
know a decent Jew, for whom I feel sorry, but the others must be
horrible!"

Anybody who wanted to recognize the full extent of the terror
had to keep his eyes open. One would think that the intellectual
class of people would have seen this; but this was by no means true
as a whole. At that time I had to learn to revise my ideas about the
role of education and intelligence in political matters. The fact is
that the intelligent person has at his disposal enough arguments
and associations to prove to himself that what he fears isn't true
at all. He is also much smarter at assessing the opportunistic
chances of getting ahead than the naïve spirits. Thus precisely in
the intellectual class one could observe lamentable examples of
character failure and delusion. In times which demand the utmost
of men, intellectual enlightenment is of very little help. The uncommitted mind, though it has been highly trained and perhaps
has even achieved the eminence of a renowned academic chair, all
too easily succumbs to the law of least resistance. The person who
insists upon maintaining his self-respect in the midst of the terror
or refusing to become an object of contempt in the face of the
hunger and dread of a concentration camp does not need to be
an "educated" man; but he must have inner reserves and commit-
ments. The best and most reliable "resisters" were to be found
among mature Christians—not among those who merely went
along with the Christian convention—and among Communists.

It follows, then, that in such a situation those who were in op-

---

[2] Here I am thinking above all of the *Stürmer*, the newspaper published
by Julius Streicher, who was executed in Nuremberg after the war.

position to the regime and also willing to engage in dangerous action could be only a widely scattered "dispersion."

And then we must remember the techniques of exercising power in an ideological tyranny which has total control. A "meeting" of the opposition is completely impossible. There were only the secret mutterings of small groups. And how many there were who went to a horrible death because of only *one* informer even in these tiny groups! And there were multitudes of such anonymous informers who either acted upon their own initiative or were systematically placed by the authorities. I must restrain myself to keep from telling you a whole string of ghastly stories of incidents which occurred within my own personal circle of experience.

Sixth: And the military? That is a chapter in itself, but I must at least give a few indications of the part it played. The German military has never yet lent itself to revolution. It has been mockingly said that the Germans could never pull off a revolution because, after all, it is forbidden to walk on the grass. And if they wanted to occupy a railroad station they would first buy a platform ticket.

In this gibe there are some indications which point to a deeper-lying circumstance. I mention only two of them.

In the first place, the officers of the German army throughout their whole tradition were always trained to be *non*political. They were to be the sword of the sovereign ruler and were sworn to personal loyalty to him. I have witnessed some dreadful spiritual struggles on the part of officers who literally had to fight their way through, or simply could not fight their way through, to the idea that their commander-in-chief was a criminal. This idea was contrary to the whole ethos which had been instilled in them and had now become second nature, contrary to all their secondary and acquired reflexes.

In line with this training in respect for the supreme representative of the state it was natural that one of the cardinal virtues of the German officer should be that of obedience. It therefore requires some imagination to visualize the demonic reversals that had to take place when this traditional virtue was exploited by a criminal and used to give impetus to his heinous activities. To override the function of swordbearer, of being only an instrument, to make personal and oppositional decisions, to act maturely and on one's own responsibility—this was reserved, at any rate in Prussian history, only to very unusual and exceptional situations. That the exception could become the rule and that resistance may be demanded as a rule—this was quite beyond the imagination of most of them.

In the *second* place, it would seem to me to be unfair to speak only of this training to slavish obedience. On several occasions Theophil Wurm, the venerable bishop of Württemberg, who was not only one of the most stanch resistance fighters but also a highly educated historian, made the following comment on this to me: "We Swabians are far more stubborn and oppositional than you Prussians. For we had a number of utterly miserable sovereigns who were always throwing into prison or exiling the best people in our country. Doing this they stirred up in us a tendency toward rebellion. And the words '*In tyrannos*' which young Schiller attached to his play *The Robbers* were sure to be received with approval and understanding. But you Prussians had too many good kings and now this is your downfall. Now people simply cannot imagine that the man in Berlin, to whom they swore allegiance as they did to old Kaiser Wilhem the First, could possibly be a scoundrel and that they must watch out lest the supreme commander play fast and loose with the oath of allegiance. It is the very greatness of the past that makes the present perversion of it so thorough and disastrous." The venerable bishop expressed it in a rather blunt and simplified way, but there is something in it. The fault is that people relied all too blindly upon men and thus surrendered their own political and ethical responsibility. And thus in the moment when they needed their sense of independence they were paralyzed.

Even the military head of the later revolt against Hitler, General von Beck—"a knight without fear or reproach"—indignantly refused as late as 1938 even to allow another highly placed general (Halder) to speak to him about a particularly shameful act of the regime and his chief: "Mutiny and revolution are words that do not exist in the vocabulary of a German soldier."[3] One can only guess how thorny was the inner path that finally led this Prussian officer to become the military head of a rebellion and to approve the attempt on Hitler's life. He too paid for it with his life. One dare not forget how many German generals thus became victims of the regime through execution, direct murder and suicide or a combination of both (as in the case of Marshal Rommel who was famous and admired even in this country).

Here I have referred to traditions of very long standing. If time were available to be exhaustive on this point, I would also have to say something about the aftereffects of Luther's theology of government and the abuse of the doctrine of the two kingdoms.[4]

Seventh: Then, as you know, it did at one point come to open rebellion—the bloodily suppressed attempt on July 20, 1944. Repeated references have been made—also in a very well-known American book—to the dilettante character of this venture which was doomed to failure. I regard this judgment itself as being very dilettante and almost intolerable, considering the sacrifices that it involved, of which I knew not a little. It only shows how little it is possible for those who live in the atmosphere of a free constitutional state to understand a resistance situation in a totalitarian country. I shall attempt by means of a very simplified example to show how hard it was to take forceful action under these circumstances.

I have already mentioned the fact that one could not openly call for resistance, that one had to be terribly cautious. Because of this need for caution there could have been only a very few who knew all the resistance groups and could have co-ordinated

[3] Gerhard Ritter, *Carl Goerdeler und die deutsche Widerstandsbewegung,* 1954, p. 146.
[4] Cf. *Theologische Ethik,* Band II, 1, §2022 ff.; Band II, 2, Index under the word *"Widerstand."*

them. We other small and young figures were aware only of minimal segments of this front.

Now any one of you can see that (with or without an attempt on the life of the Führer) it would take at least a unit of troops, however small it might be (let us say, a company), in order to knock out the Führer's headquarters. It would also take several other companies to occupy the various ministries, the radio stations, and other power centers. Let us assume that compact units numbering a total of a thousand men would have been needed. But even in an army of millions these one thousand men could not have been found; for every company was infested with so-called *N. S. Führungsoffizieren* (National Socialist Guidance Officers) and every company contained at least several sworn Nazis. They were therefore without exception unreliable for such measures. And, as it turned out, the whole thing was wrecked by the little guidance officer of the small Berlin garrison company, who smelled a rat.

At the beginning of the Third Reich, when the position of the armed forces over against Hitler was still very much stronger, the situation was not yet ripe for a military resistance. At that time the command and the troops had not yet seen which way the wind was blowing. They were still fascinated by rearmament and their gain in prestige; the new guns and aircraft, the new parade uniforms, were all too wonderful playthings. (What soldier would not be unsusceptible to this?) But later they had been lured too far into the trap to have sufficient freedom of movement.

Here again I do not wish to make it appear that the army was merely the pure and innocent object of cunning and trickery. It certainly was this, but it was not simply innocent. There are serious and balanced observers who have doubtless detected this or that opportunity when something could have been done and *no* action was taken. The last opportunity when a determined corps of officers might still have been able to do something was probably in 1938 when one of the most respected generals of the army (von Fritsch) was removed from office in a disgraceful and defamatory way. (Later he sought death on the battlefield and found it.) And though I ventured a while ago to mention the Prussian tradition of obedience as a mitigating factor, I am here obliged to use the same tradition as an indictment: to look on idly, even though angrily, while the blameless commander-in-chief of the army was stripped of his honor in the most shabby way, not to rise up against this or resign from the service—this certainly was *not* in the spirit of that tradition.

Eighth: A great hindrance to the resistance was also the fact that the troops were sworn to personal allegiance to Hitler. How few saw through the form of this oath from the beginning! How few were moved to ponder the consequences that this might lead to! The fact is, of course, that very few had seen through Hitler himself. And could those who had some presentiment avoid taking the oath? And to be prepared ultimately to break the oath or to regard oneself as having been compelled to swear an oath contrary to conscience or to regard it as null and void in the face of Hitler's gigantic perjury would have required a great deal of reflection which was left to the conscience of the solitary individual, since no one could speak about it openly or write a catechism on oaths. True, the church did say something, but it was so general that it took very little effort to miss it altogether.

Ninth: Nor can we overlook the indescribable fear of the indescribable terror. There is no such thing as mass heroism. This can be seen in the democracies too, though there the conditions that make it possible for a man to stand up for his rights are incomparably easier. But even the man who may have had some heroic impulses could very soon be gripped by cold horror. I am by no means thinking only of the ingenious tortures which were at the disposal of the hangmen and jailers—women could faint at the mere description of these things—but also of the fact that revenge was taken upon the wives and children in the form of "family arrest" (*Sippenhaft*) by torturing, imprisoning, or killing them, by depriving children of their names and spiriting them away in order to wipe out the family. The weekly radio broadcasts seeking the names of lost children which continue to this day (after almost twenty years) are the result of this horrible business.

I could continue at length, but I shall conclude the list of my main points here. Let me repeat once more what is my greatest concern. I have tried to say something that will contribute to an "understanding" of this darkest chapter in German history. This meant that I had to outline for you according to my best knowledge and conscience certain preconditions which had to be present in order to bring things to such a pass. The historical preconditions which allowed this situation to occur do not have the status of causes which explain, but rather of conditions that help one to understand. And the point is that to understand all does *not* mean to forgive all. I have had no desire to suppress or keep silent about what I consider to be our fault, even though I regard collective and wholesale confessions of guilt as being all too easy and therefore trivializing. If confessions of guilt are to be taken seriously, they must deal with specifics. This is why personal and specific confession is far harder than a general confession in which I acknowledge all my sinfulness in "thought, word, and deed." So I repeat, I have no brief for the saying "To understand all is to forgive all." Nevertheless, what I have said about the "preconditions" may perhaps contain a challenge to understand *and* to forgive when you, as citizens of another country, begin to ponder the question whether in a similar situation you would have remained without fault and therefore be justified in casting the "first stone."

But despite all the important factors which I have mentioned I should be passing over the most important reason of all for this guilt and catastrophe if I did not make the following statement: It is my firm conviction that the ultimate reason why all this could have happened is theological in nature. It consists in the major premise of the anthropology upheld by the rulers and against which the German people manifestly possessed no inner defense. That may perhaps sound somewhat mysterious, and I will explain briefly what I mean.

There are two extremely different views of man. In one I evaluate man according to his functional worth, as a working power in the production process, as the bearer of erotic attractiveness (such as sex appeal) or of biological value (for example, in the sense given it by a doctrine of the master race). At bottom this view of man is pragmatic. In normal times its destructive features are sometimes veiled, or better, disguised. As long as a person functions as a valuable labor force he may be highly esteemed and perhaps honored as a "hero of labor." Likewise his life moves on a high road, at least outwardly, as long as he functions erotically, that is, as long as he is young and attractive. And the same applies to his biological value in so far as he belongs to the "right" race and represents its supposed qualities.

This view of man which is determined by his functional value therefore contains a very definite pragmatic scale of values. This scale of values suggests the analogy of a machine. For a machine is likewise evaluated exclusively according to its functional value. If it is efficient and productive, it is, so to speak, "respected"; it is treasured and carefully serviced. When it is worn out and incapable of functioning it is scrapped. This analogy has some oppressing features when it is applied to the human parallel; for the high esteem which the efficiently functioning man enjoys in society is logically paralleled by his complete depreciation as soon as he loses his functional value. Then by a logical necessity the end result must be the concept of "life that is not worth being allowed to live." And inherent in this concept is the further logical consequence that "worthless life," like a machine which no longer functions, must be scrapped. In this case the term used is "liquidate."

We can demonstrate the truth of this logical process with some ghastly historical examples. We need only to think of the mass liquidations of the Stalinist era in Soviet Russia. As soon as it became apparent that a particular social class (such as the nobility and the middle class) could not be re-educated, i.e., sociologically repaired, they were liquidated en masse. The same procedure can be observed in the extermination of the mentally defective and of the Jews under Hitler.

It would be an all too easy oversimplification to speak of these men as "criminals." It is true, of course, that such attitudes toward human beings attract the criminal element like a magnet and that the dregs of humanity (above all, the servile opportunists and also sadists) are mobilized on a large scale in order to set in action this cynically pragmatic view of man. And yet moral and criminal categories are insufficient to plumb the depths of what . happened here. Crazy as it may sound, these gruesome characters had a code of ethics. When, for example, a member of the SS, who had been ordered to undertake a mass execution, asked for an audience with the chief of the SS (Himmler) and told him that he could not do this for reasons of conscience, the reply he received was something like this: "It is not your conscience but your weakness that recoils from the horrible. The National Socialist conscience has upon its table of laws certain supreme values such as the purity of the race. From this follows the ethical postulate that all destructive racial elements (Jews) and all inferior life which is merely a hindrance (mental defectives) must be destroyed. Here is where the moral demands which must bind your conscience are to be found. Your inhibitions lie either in your cowardice which prevents you from drawing the ethical consequences or in the fact that your conscience has not yet thrown off the remnants of bourgeois, Christian, Mediterranean ideas."

Thus Himmler—perhaps the most grotesque and abysmal figure in the Third Reich—did not reply to the SS man by saying: "You must not be so scrupulous; you sometimes have to do evil things for political reasons." On the contrary he says to him: "What I am ordering you to do is *good* according to our scale of values." And to that extent he was relatively right, since all our judgments concerning good and evil depend upon the supreme and guiding values in which we believe.

Thus it can happen that a person may come from a good family and be raised with a sense of responsibility and still may do what is wicked with a subjectively good conscience. In times when all values are changed and pitched into chaos, subjective decency and personal good-naturedness count for very little. This is why among the hangmen there were so many upright and simple citizens who after the collapse were quite able to submerge themselves and lead a blameless life as loyal workers and good fathers of families. Think of the many who are being arrested today for their crimes as they are ferreted out of their hiding places and who arouse the bewildered horror of their neighbors and acquaintances. They simply cannot comprehend that this loyal worker, who has faithfully done his duty, who has sung tender Christmas carols with his children and been a devoted friend of his dog, his cat, and his canary, could have been a mass murderer. This can be regarded as an apparent and irritating contradiction only by those who have not understood the theological background of these actions, namely, that all subjective good-naturedness goes by the board when it enters the service of a false set of values.

As a representative of a country which has gone through these truly apocalyptic experiences, one can only lift up his voice in warning and say to his friends in this far more fortunate country: Take care that mere good manners, the simple slogan "Be nice to one another," is not the ultimate determinant of your relationship to your fellow human beings. The very thing which Americans possess to such a large extent, this art of human relations, this ability to establish smooth and uncomplicated communication, can be suddenly paralyzed and turned into its opposite when we no longer know who and what man really is. Then all this "niceness" can become merely the expression of a pragmatic doctrine of optimal manners and etiquette. Then one is no longer "nice" because one has respect for human dignity, but rather because one desires merely for very practical reasons to eliminate as much as possible all friction from social intercourse and not allow any sand to get into the social machinery.

This pragmatism, ladies and gentlemen, will not stand the test if ever rulers should appear who bring to you a different set of values. Then people would not even recognize their dreadful consequences, for they can have a very pleasing exterior. These demonic figures would not have the appearance of criminals with piercing eyes, a brutal jaw, and unshaven faces. They would be pictured patting the heads of little children and fondling their dogs. They would quote Bible passages and disseminate stories of how they cannot sleep at night for concern over their people. They would come before the public as men of responsibility and moral conviction. Only one thing in them would be a little different from before: they would have a somewhat different scale of values.

But the very thing which begins so imperceptibly, which at the outset is only a slight (seemingly slight) shift in values, then becomes enlarged as with a pantograph and turns into a dreadful reality that leads to the murder, the liquidation, and the scrapping of human beings. And even then many do not see what a hideous perversion it is and they say: What do you expect? We are doing what is good; we are only carrying out a responsible program.

He who has ears, let him hear. It could be that the development of the race question in America has in it a tendency in this direction. I hope not, but it could be possible. Therefore, as one who has found in this country so much genuine and unpragmatic humanity, I have felt that I could not keep silent about the sad and guilty experience of my country but must set it before you as a warning signal.

I said a while ago that there are two extremely different views of man. We have dealt with one of them, the pragmatic view of man with its differing scale of values and its horrible consequences.

The opposite view is the one we find in the gospel. Here the dignity of man rests not upon his functional ability, but rather upon the fact that God loves him, that he was dearly purchased, that Christ died for him, and that therefore he stands under the protection of God's eternal goodness. And the mentally defective and those who are worthless in the eyes of men are also under this protection. Thus Bodelschwingh, the director of an institution for epileptics, could fling himself against the myrmidons of the SS and say: "You will take them away (for killing) only over my dead body." He knew that even the most wretched of them, in whom our human eyes can scarcely see a spark of humanity, are loved by God—and no one dares to snatch them out of his hand. They have no immanent functional value, but they do have what Luther called man's "alien dignity," which means that they have a relationship, a history with God, and that the sacrifice of God hallows them and makes them sacrosanct. Only in this "alien dignity" is there any security. In any other case we are delivered over to human evaluation and manipulation.

I believe that right here Christianity has a tremendous responsibility. I must preach this truth of man's "alien dignity." It must guard the scale of values in the name of God's commandments and the gospel. It is at this point that we make the critical decision which will affect even the most practical political developments. And here it is more evident than anywhere else that decisions of faith are more than a matter of "dogmatics" within the church, that what is here proclaimed, believed, and acted upon in obedience has its effect in the realm of actual, practical, and political decisions.

There is so much talk about the church's responsibility for society. This often means that the church must take a position with regard to social, cultural, and political questions. I would by no means deny that this is part of its obligation. But *prior* to all secondary statements of its position is the primary task of the church to proclaim and to hold before the public consciousness this major premise, this fateful premise of anthropology, this central image of humanity which is set before our eyes in the gospel.

Let me conclude by trying once more to define this fundamental and really fateful thesis (looking back as I do so to the way in which this thesis became the key principle of the darkest chapter in the history of my country). What matters is not the utilization of man but rather the infinite value of the human soul. Any emphasis upon the utilization of man delivers us over to the disposition of human hands and therefore to the most frightful manipulations. But knowing the infinite value of the human soul allows us to be secure in the hands of God. We must decide whether we shall see in man an instrument of society or a child of God. We must decide whether we want to see him delivered over to men or to the protection of God's eternal goodness.

QUESTION: What we have heard in answer to the question that was presented has been not only an interpretation of a part of German history but also a message to us Americans. I believe that now we not only have a better understanding of some things in the Hitler period which were obscure before but that we also have learned to see it in the light of the Word of God. And since the same Word has been given to us, we need to examine ourselves and ask what dark potentialities may be hidden in our country too. We shall not close our minds to this solidarity.

You must therefore not regard it as American self-righteousness if I ask you another question. You spoke of misguided obedience, especially military obedience as it was rooted in Prussian tradition and so terribly misused by Hitler. Do you really believe that aberration of this kind would be possible among us? I am really not asking this question with a pharisaic motive. I certainly do not mean that we Americans are better people, but I am only asking myself whether our democratic mind does not perhaps protect us from this blind obedience and its misuse. After all, we do not have this oath of allegiance to the head of the state as was the case with your kings. We do not think so much in terms of the state and authority as is probably true in your traditions. We are much more oriented toward society. Does not this constitute a certain safeguard?

ANSWER: I thank you for your confidence, but I am not at all sure whether I am capable of making the judgment which you apparently think I can make. And for my part, I too would be loath to be accused of pharisaism when I must answer your question not with a harmless, inoffensive statement, but rather with a criticism of American life. But since, I believe, I have not been sparing in self-criticism, you will trust that this criticism, which, after all, you have asked for, is one that is honestly addressed to *friends*. You must therefore take what I want to say not as an assertion but rather as a question addressed to you.

I too am much impressed by what you call the democratic mind of Americans. It has become quite clear to me in your country that the traditions of my country are not only in many respects great but that they are also a burden, that they not only help us to cope with life but that we must also cope with them. And yet I believe that servile, unquestioning obedience is by no means found only in certain traditions of the relation of citizen and government. It can also be generated by quite different conventions.

In this respect there are two phenomena which I have noted especially in this country, and I beg you to allow me to say this in an honest and friendly spirit.

In the first place there is in this country what is to my notion a rather remarkable obedience to certain rigid conventions of society. Here few would dare to depart from the norm. A person dare not, for example, wish to be different from others, not even in his clothing. For example, I have heard (can this really be so?) that women must not wear white shoes before Pentecost. You will know more illustrations of this law of conformism than I do, so I will refrain from giving more of them. Naturally this is true among us too, and we need only to mention the word "fashion" to have a particularly striking example. And yet in this country this seems to me to go much further and to extend to all areas of life.

The same is true with regard to obedience to the laws of the state. Perhaps it has something to do with the virute of democratic freedom that one must have a very special respect for the inviolable rule of law in order to remain in form. Now, naturally I would not advocate any softening of our attitude toward the law. Nevertheless it has struck me that the unquestioning way in which obedience is practiced in this respect can sometimes go very far. If one is not satisfied, for example, with the legal solution of the race question, even earnest Christian people shrink from the mere discussion of this question whether one must under all circumstances abide by a law which is contrary to one's conscience. For many people it is an intolerable disgrace for a respected person who has disobeyed the law for reasons of conscience to have to go to jail. A minister in jail—that simply will not do!

It is not without respect that I express the criticism implied in what I have said. The fact that the law has this status in the public mind is doubtless owing to the fact that it has generally merited this respect. And it is not a good sign when at many times in my country it was no disgrace at all for a man to be jailed for trespassing against the law. The respect which Americans show for the law doubtless lies in good part in the fact that people start with the very positive presupposition that the law of the state is good and in accord with what the conscience—including the conscience bound by faith—demands, or that at any rate it provides room for this freedom of conscience. And it is right here that I ask myself whether the process in this country could not— *mutatis mutandis*—develop further in much the same way that it did in the case of the Prussian kings. That is to say, is it not possible that people may become so *accustomed* to the goodness of the authority that they no longer really think that the law (and the "king") can fail and therefore tend to overlook possible conflicts and so allow their own responsibility of conscience to go to sleep?

Here I make bold to tell you about a rather disreputable incident which will illustrate what I mean. I would by no means generalize it; this you must believe. It certainly was a departure from the normal track. But even such a derailment can show which direction the train was going.

After the German collapse in 1945 a great many evildoers were caught by the occupation powers, but now and again they also picked up some who were really innocent. In the general chaos this probably could not be otherwise. You can imagine how many people sought revenge on others with the help of the military government and therefore how many wicked denunciations were passed on to the authorities. No wonder that in the general confusion the allied powers were not always able to distinguish the false from the true. At that time a very faithful man of one church fell victim to such a denunciation. (According to my memory he was a deacon.) He was absolutely innocent and he was highly esteemed by all honest people. The denunciation was so terrible and so cleverly contrived that he was condemned by a summary court and was facing execution. The bishop was called upon for help by the family, the congregation, and the friends of the condemned man. What I am telling you here I learned from his despairing account of what happened. The bishop knew that only a statement and appeal for reprieve to the president of the United States would be of any avail. But how could such a message reach the president? At that time there was no mail or telegraph service for Germans. It was impossible to send a letter outside the country. Only the American army could make it possible to send a letter to the president; so the bishop turned to the commanding American general of the region. He knew him to be a convinced Christian, an upright and kindly disposed man who would surely forward the letter. The general refused, however, and referred to the regulation that the American military post office was not allowed to forward any letter for Germans. We were quite aware of this regulation because it had frustrated all our attempts to communicate with our American friends, and naturally he had to understand and respect it. In this case, however, the bishop pleaded with the general to disregard the "law" because it was a question of the life of a man innocently condemned to death. This emergency, he said, transcends all rules. In his agitation the bishop could not restrain his tears and the general too was visibly moved and near to tears. But he persisted in his refusal. He could not act against his orders, he said. (I think I also remember that he pointed out the consequences that such an offense would have for him, but of this I am no longer absolutely sure.) So he refused to accept the bishop's letter. Thereupon the bishop could not refrain from saying to the general: "Quite apart from the blood of this innocent man, I must point out to you that you are now doing the very thing which has prompted you to make yourselves judges of the blind obedience of the German public. Take care lest you end up in exactly the same place where we are today."

As I have said, I am guarding against any kind of generalization; I am not saying that this is the way "the" Americans act, that this is how they enslave themselves to the letter of the law. This extreme case is intended only to illustrate certain possibilities which can happen here too, if no room is left for the possibility of having to say, "Here I stand, I cannot do otherwise." This possibility must be there with regard to any law however greatly it may be respected. And this possibility *can* exist only if our personal conscience is bound to the ultimate court of appeal which is God, and only if it remains alert, sensitive, and independent in this ultimate dependence upon God.

I could tell you of many other incidents of this terrible period which point to the same unfathomable depths. I shall not do so, however, for I do not want to give even the appearance of wanting to set off fault against fault. We must not judge one another but rather help one another. And besides, if we once undertook to balance accounts against one another we would finally find ourselves back with Adam and Eve and her grasping for the forbidden fruit.

QUESTION: Though you have shown us the background against which the disastrous development in Germany must be seen, I still

cannot believe that these mass murders could have happened if
the German people had *known* these things. I can understand that
at the beginning there was no protest because the new rulers disguised their real intentions. But I cannot believe that if they had
had a clear knowledge of what was happening, they would have
tolerated the deportation and the gassing of millions of people.
I have repeatedly been assured by German friends that they really
knew nothing about this, and that when they learned of it after the
war it was a horrible shock to them. Considering the magnitude
of the crime, I cannot understand how it could have remained
a secret.

But my friends are absolutely trustworthy. And I also *wanted*
to believe them, because it upheld my faith in the German people.
Otherwise one could lose confidence in all of them. And then,
despite everything you have said, we would still have to raise the
question: How could such a thing have been possible among the
"people of poets and thinkers"? So I ask you: Did the Germans
know all this or not?

ANSWER: I could take the relatively easy way out and answer your
question by saying that at any rate, of the people whom I know,
not one knew the full extent of what happened. But naturally a
great many must have caught some sound of the beating wings of
darkness circling above us; rumors of what was happening were
going around. But there was nothing to take hold of because the
things themselves were done in secrecy and were also carefully
concealed by the authorities. It was possible to dismiss all these
rumors and to say to oneself: "I have no use for rumors" (which
in normal times may be a perfectly honorable point of view).
Moreover, many well-bred, decent people said to themselves:
"This simply cannot be true; such infamy is beyond all imagination." People said to themselves the very same thing that you have
just said: "How could such a thing be possible at all in our country?" The daily propaganda kept drumming it into people's heads
that the "enemy stations" were broadcasting the most absurd lies
in order to "break down our fighting strength." And many at-

tributed the rumors of atrocities to enemy psychological warfare the purpose of which was to break down morale. It is true that the star of David was to be seen in the streets. It would have taken some effort of imagination to visualize the misery of those who were compelled to wear it, but this people preferred not to do, for they were already sufficiently burdened with anxiety about the next night of bombing, with care for the future and for their husbands and sons at the front. I myself knew considerably more than most because I had access to something more than just everyday sources of information and because many of my friends were directly affected. Nor did I myself come off unscathed, and very early I learned to know some partial aspects of the bestiality of the rulers. But I too did not even remotely suspect the full extent of what was happening around us. And I do not consider it out of the question that I too would have thought it impossible if someone had told me about it before 1945. And after all, I was one who thought the Nazis were capable of some pretty outrageous things.

So I could answer your question with relative ease by saying that the Germans quite generally did not know the magnitude of the abominations. Many heard only rumors of some horrible doings, but did not believe them.

And yet, though there would be something right in that statement, I would still have the feeling that I was not being altogether truthful if I were to leave it at that. I believe that I was in duty bound first to set before you *this* view of the matter, for the American people with their free press, their open criticism, and democratic lack of constraint in which one can discuss all political questions simply cannot imagine to what extent a controlled and censored press, a managed and manipulated radio broadcasting system, and a subtly contrived strategy of mass suggestion can produce an almost impenetrable smoke screen.

Why is it that despite all this I would not have a good conscience if I spoke only of the fact that the Germans did not know what was going on? Well, there are two different ways of not-knowing. One consists in the fact that one really has no information whatsoever and therefore *cannot* know anything. The other has its root in the fact that one does not *want* to know something, that one is therefore *repressing* something which might possibly be known. And I cherish the conviction that innumerable Germans—particularly in such responsible positions as the higher military echelons, for example—repressed the truth about the terror which was accessible to them. Apart from the top functionaries of the system, the entire extent of the terror was doubtless unknown to anyone. But those crimes that were known were quite horrible enough to have forced us to see that we had fallen into the hands of men who had run amuck on a tremendous scale. And it was precisely these partial aspects of the dreadful truth which were repressed. They were not allowed to enter into our consciousness. And to this extent it is not altogether false when many today say: "We knew nothing about it." When they say this, they are not telling an absolute lie.

But *then* does not the fault lie precisely in those acts of repression? Were they not cowardly acts of evasion and flight? Did they not mean a retreat from the responsibility that was required?

This question must certainly be answered in the affirmative. The only question is whether one can answer it affirmatively in the pharisaic sense that "I" would have faced the truth unconditionally. Perhaps I can say something about how these things look "from the inside," because I lived through this time as a pastor who spoke to and listened to very many and very different kinds of people. And for this reason I also tried to get in touch with a number of men in responsible positions in order to form a group which would concern itself with an intellectual and spiritual plan for a new beginning after the expected collapse of the Hitler era. In these contacts I had to talk with them concerning the horrible (partial) truths about which I knew. Again and again I met with resistance, and I also observed how many avoided any contact with me in order not to be confronted with these problems.

Why did these men evade the issue? Was it because of cowardice?

I now appeal for a moment to your imagination.

Think of a general who has come home for a brief furlough from the increasingly wavering front in the battlefields of the Soviet Union. The pressures and impressions of the hardships, the daily bloodshed, and the secret dread of the growing Soviet superiority of power are almost overwhelming him. And then you try to tell him something of the crimes of the regime at home and in the occupied countries. You try to tell him considerately that his commander-in-chief is a madman. Assume that he would not forthwith dismiss any thought of this kind because of his officer's tradition and refuse to listen to such talk because of his oath of allegiance. Try to think of this general simply as a *man*, a man to whom the lives of thousands of men, a division, or an army are committed. How would he react to such news?

The dreadful responsibilities he must bear, the sacrifices of hardship and blood he must demand of his men—this can be borne only if he sees some meaning and purpose in it. And he can see meaning in it only if he is convinced that he is protecting the homeland from the Red flood and that the supreme representatives of his homeland—in whose service he stands—are worthy of that trust. If he came to the conviction that this war was not a defensive war at all, but that Hitler had started it in pursuit of his insane notions of world conquest, that Hitler himself was a prince of darkness and a madman, and that the homeland which he thought he was defending in Hitler's name was actually being *destroyed* by his government, that therefore all the values which he was fighting for would go to the dogs anyhow—assuming that he came to this conviction, I ask you, how could he bear the burden of such knowledge? This would not only take away all meaning from his struggle and that of his men, it would not only reduce every sacrifice to horrible futility, but it would also confront him with some very definite consequences. Could he go on allowing himself to be used by this villain, could he go on serving him? Would not this mean that he was making himself a party to this gigantic work of destruction and murder?

Let us assume further that the general had fought his way through to this question and was willing to face the consequences. Then he would have to face the question whether he should quit the service. An official resignation would certainly not be accepted. Therefore he would have to flee and become a "defeatist." And here I will set aside the very important question of what this would mean for his family, upon whom the regime would take revenge in the form of "family arrest" or even more horrible reprisals. I am thinking now only of his own role. So he would have to flee. But where? In practice this could only mean going over to the enemy. For the dreadful thing about totalitarian tyrannies is that they recognize no wildernesses into which an opponent can be exiled or to which he might flee. Not even a wilderness any more! Do you understand what that means? But then can he go over to the Bolsheviks? Do not they present a threat which is at least as abominable as the terror of Hitlerism? And quite apart from that, would he not have to condemn himself for disloyalty to the soldiers entrusted to him? They would have to endure cold, hunger, and hardship and die like flies, since they had no chance whatsoever to escape. And if he left, who would take his place? Perhaps one of Himmler's functionaries?

I have had to demand this brief and probably very depressing meditation from your imagination in order to show the utter hopelessness and despair of a general who looked the situation straight in the eye. And we can understand why he did *not* look at it straight in the eye, but rather repressed the truth. If he had dared to look at the truth, he would have been obliged either to draw the consequences or to go on performing his service contrary to his convictions. Then he would have delivered himself to the accusation of his conscience—an accusation which would have been all the more dreadful because he could not allow his distress to be seen. (He would have to play the strong man in addresses to the troops, in issuing the orders of the day, and in his staff conferences; for to go on as before and at the same time undermine morale would be complete madness.)

So he flees through repression into not-knowing in order at least to preserve the illusion of subjective decency. He seeks to salvage a certain ethos which he needed for his self-respect. He does his duty. He spends himself in performing his responsibility to carry out orders and he evades the responsibility of decision. He shuts his eyes when the question in whose name and for whom and for what he is fighting threatens to become overwhelming.

Many ordinary Germans certainly would not have been confronted with this degree of helplessness; and the fact is that there were prominent officials in no small number who would not have found it so hard at least to have accepted *certain* insights and *certain* consequences. But I have purposely chosen the most difficult case. And I have purposely chosen a general as an illustration, because people abroad tend to put the *greatest* blame upon this species of men.

I personally encountered many such conflicts, however, among those in the lower ranks, young officers and soldiers. Many of my students were officers. They fought on all the fronts, and on their furloughs they would come to me and ask, "What's going on here at home? We have been hearing some things." At first I always told them the plain truth, but then it cut my heart to have to let them go away in despair, having now to bear the inner burden of this knowledge on top of the burden of the battlefield. I can still hear the despairing cry of a young officer-theologian: "What then are we fighting for, if this fellow is destroying our church?" Another had tears in his eyes because he could not bear the thought that he was sworn to Hitler while his father was in prison as a Confessing pastor. Both of them were killed in battle. Only a few of my young students of that time ever returned. And I know that several of them sought death because they could not endure the contradiction. A young half-Jew, for example, one of the most faithful and gifted of them all, volunteered for every possible dangerous patrol duty. He knew far more than he could bear. And one day he did not have to come back.

So at first I told my young visitors what was afoot. Later I abstained, evaded the question, and even trivialized it. I could no longer bear it. Their burden was heavy enough as it was. The burden of knowing the truth in addition would have crushed them.

Finally, one thing more. Surely there are no fewer honest, upright people among us than among you, fathers and mothers who care for their families and do their duty, young idealists and mature, balanced old people. Certainly our people do not consist *only* of such persons, any more than does the American people; but thank God, they do exist in no small numbers. And these ordinary decent people often refused to believe these outrages because they seemed inconceivable to them. They simply could not comprehend it; their imagination was not cynical enough.

Do you now have the impression that I have been trying to trivialize the whole thing? Please do not think so! Anybody who has listened at all must surely have noted where I have put the accent in this question of guilt. I admit that it is not without fear that I have done so. For the guilt that we are dealing with *here*, the guilt which was incurred in repressing the truth, is no cheap and superficial, no mere "moral" guilt. It lies deeper and is more subtle. When I have spoken to my people at home the accent has sometimes been put elsewhere. But with you here in America I have been primarily concerned to create an understanding of the exceeding difficulty of a situation in which the truth was hard to come by. Anybody who has experienced the difficulty of such a situation fears to have to make judgments, at any rate judgments of a general kind. He waits for the Last Judgment before which we must *all* appear. There the line between the sheep and the goats will be drawn at points which are different from what we in our myopia (and also in our moral blindness) imagine. But all speculations about this line need not worry us as long as we do not lose this one certainty: that we have one who intercedes for us in this Judgment and that the judge is our Father.

QUESTION: Is it true that the collapse of Germany in 1945 brought about a religious revival? If so, has this revival continued? If not, why did it not come or why did it cease?

ANSWER: It is exceedingly difficult to say anything about a revival and the course it may have taken. After all, what really happens in people's hearts and therefore what is spiritual or merely psychological emotion remains hidden from human eyes.

This much is certain, however, and that is that after the collapse people in Germany went through a period of tremendous shock. When everything that had happened came out and countless people were suddenly and in very different ways led into a great silence (either into the troubled silence of the new situation under the occupation or the dreadful silence of the new concentration camps), the majority undoubtedly felt that a tremendous judgment had fallen upon us. Many people even spoke of the "blessing of the zero hour," the time when things have hit absolute bottom and God gives the chance of a new beginning in the midst of the ruins and the dead. I cannot here analyze the whole complex of feelings and existential experiences which filled us at that time, and yet I dare say that the general feeling was that of visitation and judgment.

Externally this was apparent in the fact that the churches were crowded and that people literally cried out to the church for some word which would explain and point the way out of the situation. In this hour we also established the evangelical academies which sought on the basis of the gospel to point out roads to a new order and to a new self-understanding in the previously ideological country which had suddenly become a no man's land. It appeared to be a precious and fruitful hour in our history. The soil of men's hearts had been plowed and there was great readiness to repent. And there were times when I thought that now the hour of awakening might have come. Anybody who lived through these hours in the pulpit was moved by the way in which people listened.

And yet this hour, this *kairos*, passed by; people ate and drank, married and were given in marriage—and everything remained as it had always been. Why was this so? We dare not answer this with speculations and psychologizing. We have no right to specify the exact reasons why the manifest grace of God was again withdrawn from us.

And it seems to me to be clear in what direction we should look for these reasons, namely, in the direction of human guilt and human failure.

I believe, for example, that the church at that time did not find the message for the hour. There were some very unpleasant "seizures of power" and self-assertion on the part of the "old guard." Not infrequently services were rewarded with offices and occasionally someone who really had exceptional charismatic gifts was made an ecclesiastical bureaucrat, where he naturally failed. Instead of the preaching of repentance and salvation we had the proclamation of a collective guilt and a hysteria of self-accusation which was in need of psychological understanding rather than having any theological justification, and this led to a hardening of men's hearts. Despite the times, from many pulpits we heard only very conventional, pallid sermons which did not reach men's hearts and left them cold. We seemed to be denied a prophetic awakening.

But from a totally different and altogether unexpected side there came something which in my judgment constituted an obstruction in the spiritual situation. When I speak here of the procedures of denazification as they were handled particularly by the Americans, I beg you to believe that today I can speak about this completely without anger. I have long since realized that a military government coming in from the outside simply could not understand certain things in an occupied country and that this was not changed by the fantastic amounts of printed information materials which the army carried with it. At that time (1947) I preached a sermon about and against these forms of denazification which was later published along with a polemical exchange of letters[5] and also reprinted in American papers. It was precisely the reaction of American Christians to this that so happily showed me how innately helpful, fair, and self-critical people are in this country.

What was the matter with those forms of denazification?

If I may express it in rather rough and simplified form, I will put it this way. The Americans at first regarded the entire German people—with only a few exceptions—as one band of more or less thoroughgoing Nazis. Figuratively speaking they had the whole German people fall in three deep and then ordered everybody who had had anything whatsoever to do with the Party to step to the left. They then added to this group a rather large number of other people. In Württemberg, for example, this included everybody who had a title that ended with ". . . rat," such as Studienräte, Regierungsräte, Veternärräte (schoolmasters, government counselors, veterinarians). It was thought that these people must have had a specially close connection with the system. Many thousands were sent into concentration camps. Since I had suffered some unpleasantness during the Third Reich, I was among the few men who were allowed by American permission to visit these camps and could speak to those who were interned in them. There I learned to know something about the inward and the outward state of affairs. Here I am concerned only with the inward attitude of people.

The fact that very many were unjustly deprived of their positions and a good portion of them were imprisoned in itself led to a certain hardening of mind. Also contributing to this was perhaps the fact that many people had placed high hopes in liberation by the Americans, that they looked upon them as representatives of a Christian nation which would proceed in love and justice to show a nation of neopagans what true humanity is.

[5] Die Schuld der anderen (Göttingen: Vanderhoeck & Ruprecht, 1948).

In the face of such hopes any disillusionment would be sorely felt and would result in a loss of prestige for—a wrongly understood—Christianity.

But far worse than this and something which really brought with it what we have called a spiritual obstruction was the following. Innumerable people—I believe the greater part of the German people—were therefore dismissed from their jobs and professions. (At that time one could see formerly wealthy businessmen and high officials performing the manual labor of cleaning up the streets and rubble heaps.) In order to get back their positions and a livelihood, they had to undergo a process of denazification which required a testimonial. These testimonials were called *Persilscheine* (Persil was a well-known soap company which advertised that its soap would produce dazzling white laundry). The consequence was that everybody who was affected sat down and wrote letters to every possible irreproachable non-Nazi begging him to testify that he had had only a formal relationship to the Party, that he had really gone out of his way to protect the Jews, that he had always been cursing Hitler, and that he had just missed by a hair being sent to a Gestapo prison or concentration camp. And because the non-Nazis had sympathy for the many who were now being unjustly punished, they quite willingly handed out these *Persilscheine* (hopefully not too many to those who were really guilty!). Then these people could read some heart-moving words about their innocence, their heroism, their secret martyrdom. And all along we were all guilty and should have been arrested (if not by men then certainly by God). Many people had ten, twenty, and more such testimonials. Never in their lives had they seen such a flattering picture of themselves, since this is the kind of thing you read only in death notices and memorial addresses. When a man read this stuff he was able to recover his self-conceit!

Can you imagine what this method of denazification meant inwardly, "spiritually"? A people who seemed to be just at the point of grasping its guilt and should have been hearing the message of forgiveness were suddenly carried away by a gigantic stream of self-justification. It did not require the "blood of the Lamb" to rise "white as snow" from the water of reconciliation. No, the thing got washed automatically, gleaming white—with Persil!

There are many books on the history of the church in postwar Germany. They tell of *Kirchentagen* and evangelical academies, of synods and addresses to the congregations. But hardly anywhere can one read anything about the inner history of those years and nowhere is there anything about this "spiritual obstruction" (at least I have not come across it). Therefore I wanted for once to give an account of how I must look at all this. I have quite simply told you a bit of postwar history as I myself experienced it, since you asked me whether there had been a "revival."

I say all this not in order to throw the blame on the Americans of that time. It is not my business here to draw up an account of guilt. I know what *I* did that was wrong. I too wrote *Persilscheinen* until my fingers were sore in order to save as many as possible whom I considered relatively harmless sinners. But should I not have enclosed a pastoral letter which would have said to the recipient: "We are all guilty and in need of the forgiveness which no appeal board can give us"? Should I not have written to him: "I seek to wash you clean before men, but what will happen to both of us when we stand before the Last Judgment and we are asked to give an account of the years past"? "It is our guilt that we are still living," said Karl Jaspers. This may sound a bit overpathetic, but there is something to it.

We have all, each in his own way, contributed to that "spiritual obstruction." And yet there is no value in making merely general, wholesale confessions of sin. If the confession of guilt is to be taken seriously, it must be very specific and personal. The ultimate personal and specific distinctions will be made at the Last Judgment. My purpose has been, and could only be, merely to indicate what these distinctions mean here by illustrating from my own experience something of recognizable guilt. If God does not grant an awakening, then we can never simply say that he has denied us his grace. No, rather we must always confess that it is we ourselves who are blocking God's way to us.

In closing I can only thank you for having shown such fraternal interest in the fortune of my country. We have not forgotten that it was the Christians—and especially the American Christians —who stretched out their hands to us after the war and provided us and our children with food and clothing. All of us who went through those years will treasure in our hearts this act of helping love. During these last several hours which have evoked in me so many moving memories, I have felt a great gratitude that it has been possible to speak to Christians as I have here to you. Here there has been no need politely to retouch the picture or to beat about the bush. Nor does shame need to keep us from speaking. For we can take even the most painful things and set them down in the light of eternity in which we all stand together. We face one another not as strangers but as brothers. This is what I shall never forget about these hours.

IX

What Is the Most Important Question of Our Time?

A DISCUSSION WITH JOURNALISTS AND STUDENTS[1]

QUESTION: What do you consider the most important question of our time?

ANSWER: This country is proud of its standard of living, its democratic freedom, its civilizing goods, and above all its technological skills. I consider it a question of fundamental import—a question which will have real political consequences—whether we men of today learn to distinguish between what makes our existence pleasanter and easier *and* what it was created to be, what can be called its real theme.

All these civilizing goods—from television to supermarkets—are merely means which smooth our path through the world and make it easier to travel. But what will it profit us, if we make smooth social and technical progress on this level road and no longer know *where* we are going, in whose *name* we are living, and what the *goal* of our destiny is? For then perfectionism in the way in which we master life leads precisely to a life which has not been mastered. Then we shall be wandering aimlessly over a smooth and level plain.

May it not be that our neuroses and our predilection for psychiatrists derive from the fact that we have become a heap of misery

[1] The following question, which perhaps only in America is asked with such sovereign aplomb, was put to me several times in press conferences and discussions with students. It was the first question newsmen put to me upon my arrival and it came up again at my departure.

in this great empty plain? What good are our refrigerators, what good is the well-oiled apparatus of our style of living, if we no longer know what we are living for?

Albert Einstein once said that we live in an age of perfect means and confused ends. The question which is inherent in that statement I consider to be the most important question of our times. It has to do with the boredom which is deadly, with the emptiness which frightens us, but also with the fulfillments which make life worth living. It has to do with the crucial task which has been set for us, namely, to distinguish between the "means," which make our life *easier*, and the "meaning" of our life, which is the only thing that makes life *possible*. Even the person who has perfectly solved the problem of the means can still perish in suicide because a life without meaning is dreadful. And this dreadfulness actually increases as the outward course of this life grows smoother.

I can express what I mean by this as a Christian in the words of our Lord: "What will it profit a man, if he gains the whole world and forfeits his life?" All the means of mastering the world can turn a man into a fool if he overlooks the crucial question. That this should *not* happen, I consider the most important question of our time.

QUESTION: We Americans probably will hear what you have just said with a special clarity. But in principle it also applies to all the other civilized countries of the world, that is, to all nations which are in danger of expecting *everything* from the progress of their standard of living. I would like to know which question you consider the most important especially in America.

ANSWER: I could answer that very simply by saying: the race question. Though I am not a politician, I would not feel that in giving this answer I would be overstepping the competence of a theologian; for in previous statements on this question I have tried to show how deeply it touches the foundations of the Christian faith and also the human conscience. Nevertheless I cannot be content with this answer; for I believe that no traveler needs to point out to Americans the importance of this question. The mature, thinking citizens of this country know about this themselves.

I would rather—if you will permit me to make a judgment—mention an entirely different problem as being the most important question which you are facing. Not a single person ever raised it in any discussion I had in this country (it would therefore appear that people are astonishingly unconscious of it); and whenever I raised it myself, it seemed to evoke a kind of disconcerted amazement, I might almost say, a kind of embarrassment, which was probably the reason why nobody ever broached the subject. I mean the question of how Americans deal with *suffering*. Yes, you have heard aright; I mean the problem of suffering. If I have not been totally blind on this journey, I believe I have seen that Americans do not have this color on their otherwise so richly furnished palette.

Let me explain what I mean by this rather surprising statement. The question of suffering, it seems to me, appears in the lexicon of Americans only at the place where the things which are to be overcome are discussed. The American is a person who wants to solve all problems and is also quite wonderfully convinced that he can solve them. And there is no doubt that with this nerve and nonchalance he actually does succeed in solving an infinite number of things. The world owes a great deal to these qualities that Americans possess. I have no intention of indulging only in carping criticism!

But this creative nerve and this faith that everything can be solved also have their reverse side. There are some burdens in life which simply cannot be eliminated. These burdens obviously pitch the American into such helpless embarrassment that he either capitulates to them or represses them or glosses them over. And here I am thinking above all of the burdens of death and suffering.

Even the wonderful passion for improving the world cannot banish death from the world. And in this country I have always been somewhat startled by the way in which people do not dare to admit and face what they have not come to terms with. And undoubtedly people do not admit death and growing old.

Even though the notorious cemetery in Hollywood is certainly an extreme example of this absence of a relationship to death, it is nevertheless symbolic. Here—quite in line with the program of the founder—there was established a garden of life in which it would take very sharp eyes to discover even the trace of a grave. I shall not pile up any further illustrations of the same thing. You know what I mean. And you also know what I am alluding to when I say that this obvious helplessness over against the fact of death also expresses itself in the analogous refusal to recognize another fact, namely, the fact that we must grow older. This too people find hard to admit and therefore they seek to prolong their youth.

But above all, it seems to me, all this leads to a wrong attitude toward suffering. Again and again I have the feeling that suffering is regarded as something which is fundamentally inadmissible, distressing, embarrassing, and not to be endured. Naturally we are called upon to combat and diminish suffering. All medical and social action is motivated by the perfectly justified passion for this goal. But the idea that suffering is a burden which can or even should be fundamentally and radically exterminated can only lead to disastrous illusions. One perhaps does not even have to be a Christian to know that suffering belongs to the very nature of this our world and will not pass away until this world passes away. And beyond this, we Christians know that in a hidden way it is connected with man's reaching for the forbidden fruit, but that God can transform even this burden of a fallen world into a blessing and fill it with meaning.[2]

It is therefore inherent in man's very lot and being that suffering exists. That remains. So it is not only a matter of our having the task of eliminating it but also of our task of accepting it.

To me it seems that infinitely much depends upon whether

[2] Cf. the story of the healing of the man born blind, John 9:1 ff.

we learn to understand and accept this task. The degree to which we acknowledge this or fail to do so will demonstrate itself in the way in which we master life or are shipwrecked by it. And all of this must inevitably make itself apparent in the fate of a nation, indeed, of a whole generation.

It is, for example, a kind of "suffering" for the young person to have become awakened to sex and still have to spend years of maturing before he can find the fulfillment of his sexuality in a life relationship. I have come to know far too many decent young people in America, who find joy in the fashioning of their lives, to be taken in by the articles you find in papers and magazines which talk as if the colleges were nothing but theaters of promiscuity and premarital intercourse. But I also have the impression that the younger generation is quite generally at a loss about sexuality. Naturally, a certain degree of this helplessness exists always and everywhere. What I mean in this connection is more their helplessness with regard to the *obligations* of sexuality (not to speak of the *fulfillment* of this obligation).

To many it appears incomprehensible that one must endure the pains of growing, maturing, and waiting and that this is actually a meaningful obligation. And because it is incomprehensible, they do not even begin to shoulder this task but rather act according to the law of least resistance. Everybody in this country seems to be crying about this; there is no other complaint which I heard so often from anxious and lovingly concerned adults. And it seems to me that for the most part the remedy is being sought in the wrong place, namely, in lessons, warnings, and explanations which they think should be given in the realm of sex. I consider this wrong and fruitless because the trouble belongs in a larger context and can be approached only in this larger framework. If the young person sees that we are very generally unwilling to bear any pain at all, that there are pills and anodynes for everything, that we will not endure even a touch of tiredness but even here must resort to pep pills, then right from the start he cannot understand why he should endure the pressure of his sexual vitality and struggle with it. At the very point where he is most hard pressed and where he is faced with the frightening and yet fascinating alternative of pain or pleasure, why should he be willing to endure the pain and console himself with the mere hope that these abstentions will pay off? Why should he not take advantage of the obvious techniques (you see, I am avoiding the word "love") which have been developed for the premarital sexual thirst of young people?

Here, I believe, we have an adumbration of this general inability to face suffering. This is, I think, only a special instance of the fact that people have disregarded the theme of suffering, which is a fundamentally human theme, and have refused to face and accept it.

This also explains another thing—and this goes far beyond the bounds of America and I could just as well apply it to my own country—the fact that generally people see nothing wrong when the press reports that a mother has killed her incurably ill child or that a woman who is afraid of giving birth to a sick child allows the fetus to be taken from her. Do you still remember the monstrous judgment of innocence handed down by the court in Brussels? Do you remember the clamor of approval from ostensible sympathizers which in cases like this appears in the "letters to the editor" columns of the newspapers? We must guard against simply turning up our noses at such things and pride ourselves on our more respectable convictions. This could be merely a relic of our upbringing or a symptom of a moral self-assurance. We must find out exactly what it is that arouses our indignation here. For the *only* thing that justifies our protest is that we know that wherever these criminal assaults are made upon the incurable there has been a loss of knowledge of what suffering is, the meaning there is in it, and the obligations it imposes upon us. The point is that man, unlike the animals, is capable of ethical suffering. And because it has meaning it has its dignity, its value, its purpose. Therefore the *coup de grâce* may be given to an animal but not to a human being.

I have chosen only two illustrations to show what a range the problem of suffering has and how it affects the normal and the border-line situations of our life. In the face of such situations we ought to become aware of how devastating can be the illusion that we can banish suffering from the world and that its extermination is the only task it presents to us. We must try to learn again that suffering must also be accepted, that it is sent to us and laid upon us, and that thus it is one of the "pounds" with which we must "trade" (Luke 19:13). We Christians know from the gospel to what extent suffering is a raw material from which God wants to make something. We are not Prometheus who thought himself like God, who thought he could do anything and returned every package of suffering with the stamp "Acceptance refused." No, we are the people who must learn from an ancient Book to say, "Nevertheless I am continually with thee."

I wish for America, which I love very much, that it may find a new way to a willingness to understand and to accept suffering and that God may preserve it from destructive illusions.

Index

"alien dignity," man's, 164
American Christianity, xv, xvi, 17 f., 19, 130, 131
anthropomorphism, 4, 5
anxiety, 30
Apostles' Creed, 77
Athanasian Creed, 95
Augsburg Confession, 95, 132
Augustine, 8, 38

Bach, Johann Sebastian, 146
Barth, Karl, 65
Beck, General von, 155 f.
Beethoven, 146
Bernanos, Georges, 105
biblical criticism, 1, 14 ff.
Bismarck, 130
Bodelschwingh, Friedrich von, 103, 164
Bonhoeffer, Dietrich, 82
Bultmann, Rudolf, 15 f., 19 ff., 29, 31 33, 44 ff., 52, 65, 67

church, 3, 10, 13, 16 f., 21, 25 f., 28, 65, 82, 112 ff., 124 ff., 132, 142, 164
Confessing Church, 21, 147
cosmology, cosmogony, 7, 29, 31
Council of Trent, 97
creation, 7, 26, 29

Dannhauer, J. C., 39
death, 68, 110, 185
deideologizing, 116
democracy, 124, 165 f.
demythologizing, 8
denazification, 178 ff.

Dilthey, Wilhelm, 40, 148
Docetism, 9, 85, 91
dogma, 59 ff., 63 f.
doubt, 60 ff.

Einstein, Albert, 184
Enlightenment, xv, 17
epistemology, 56 ff.
eschaton, 73
ethics, 115, 132, 136
evangelical academies, 144, 177, 181
existential, 22, 36, 74, 134

faith, 6 ff., 21, 29, 33 f., 38, 42 f., 45, 48, 53, 60 ff., 75, 78 ff., 82 f., 86, 88, 95 f., 107
fate, 84, 148
forgiveness of sins, 72 f.
Fritsch, General von, 157
fundamentalism, xv, xvi, 14 ff., 60

Galen, Bishop Count von, 143
Gerstenmaier, Eugen, 141 f.
glossolalia, 88 ff.
God
  condescension of, 10, 13, 68 f., 85
  faithfulness of, 4, 61 f.
  first cause, 108
  grace of, 6, 35 ff., 97
  humanity of, 8
  personal, 5
  sovereignty of, 6, 12
  wholly other, 40
Goerdeler, Carl, 156
Goethe, 147
Goppelt. Leonhard, 46, 67
gospel, 13, 50, 65, 111, 133, 140, 163